Speci

JUNE ANN MONKS

Heartline
Books

Published by Heartline Books Limited in 2001

First published in the United Kingdom in 2001
by Heartline Books Limited.

Heartline Books Limited
PO Box 22598, London W8 7GB

Heartline Books Ltd. Reg No: 03986653

ISBN 1-903867-28-2

Styled by Oxford Designers & Illustrators

Printed and bound in Great Britain by
Cox & Wyman, Reading, Berkshire

For
Tristan and Hannah

JUNE ANN MONKS

A vivid imagination coupled with a passion for reading and writing led to June embarking on a writing career. Short stories and humorous articles came first but romantic fiction was always her first love and when her children became independent she began to write novels.

Every woman has a hero in her life and June's husband Ian will always be hers. Together they have lived all over Queensland as Ian carved out a career in the bank.

Always happy to try new experiences June has been hot air ballooning and paragliding over the sea but has bowed to family pressure to forget the parachute jump.

Readers have told us that they really love SECOND TIME AROUND, June's first book for Heartline. If you would like to read *that* book, please send a cheque or postal order to the value of £4.50 (£3.99 plus p&p), to us at P O Box 22598, London W8 7GB, and we'll be pleased to send you the book by return.

chapter one

Two babies in a basket. Nicholas Best stared down at his doorstep in disbelief. He closed his eyes and then opened them cautiously. The basket and its small occupants hadn't disappeared.

He ran a hand through his hair. He hadn't been drinking. Hell! It was only nine o'clock in the morning. Desperately trying to organise his thoughts into some sort of order, he glanced around. Babies didn't land on doorsteps without help and he had answered the strident ringing of the door-bell. Someone had performed both tasks and they couldn't have gone far.

They hadn't.

Grace Palmer peered around the corner of the old shed. She ducked back when she saw Nicholas Best lift his head and give the landscape a searching glance. He was still in her line of vision and she watched anxiously, hoping that he wouldn't enlarge his search to the surrounding trees where her car was hidden.

As he gazed around she could sense his feeling of help-lessness. That must be a first for a man who had a reputa-tion for taking life into his hands, and moulding it to his own needs. She shivered as she reminded herself that he had used Karen ruthlessly – and without any thought for the consequences of his actions.

A wry smile twisted her mouth as she glanced towards the basket containing the twins. Some consequence! And then the smile faded as she wondered if she was doing the wrong thing?

She drew in a deep breath. It had been a heart-rending decision. Oblivious to the danger of being seen, she peered around the shed to take a better look at the man who had fathered her sister's children.

Her breath whooshed into her lungs in dismay. He was *huge*! She tried to rationalise her reaction as she ran her eyes over his tall frame. She estimated that he must be about six foot three inches, only about a head taller than herself, but his shoulders were broad and he was quite heavily built. Perhaps it was just the fact that she was so thin and exhausted at the moment, which made almost everyone else look as if they had a much firmer grip on life.

He stepped out on to the small porch and bent down to have another look at the basket. Shafts of sunlight caught his black hair, giving it a glossy sheen like the wings of a raven. He straightened up and she noted with surprise a silver streak running through his dark hair, which gave a slightly piratical and devilish look. Even from this distance he appeared to be extremely tough and ruthless.

Grace tried to determine what it was about him that bothered her. Maybe he really *was* the Devil? She smiled grimly at her own fantasy as her hands clenched nervously into fists at her side. Was it so fantastic? From all that Karen had said, he'd sounded really evil. Her imagination went into overdrive as she pictured him in Satan's image. A devil of a man – and she'd been foolish enough to leave her sister's babies on his doorstep…?

Flying from her hiding place, Grace rushed across the uneven grass. No way was she leaving those precious twins in the care of such a man!

Nicholas' head snapped up. Ah! The culprit, he told himself, his thoughts in chaos. Why was this happening to him? If some unmarried, teenage mother was trying to foist her babies on to someone – why choose him? He knew nothing about babies and the thought of fatherhood had always filled him with horror.

As his stunned brain finally came back on track, the pieces fell into place. He had bought the old farm from Jean Bryce. Now *there* was a typical grandmother figure. Yes! The babies were definitely intended for her.

'Nicholas Best?'

The willowy, redheaded female who was now standing in front of him promptly sent his smart theory straight down the plug hole. Because, she clearly seemed to know precisely who she wanted.

Lord – she looked as if a puff of wind would blow her away! He threw a glance at the woman confronting him, before turning to look down again at the twins. No way could she have produced the two robust babies in the basket.

Another quick glance…and his eyes almost bulged from their sockets. *One of the babies had bright red hair.* So much for his ability to assess the frailty of the human form!

'Who wants to know?'

His eyes narrowed as she wiped her hands down her jeans. She was nervous. So she damned well should be, trying to foist the results of her indiscretions on to him.

'Karen Palmer's sister.'

Karen! Suddenly thoughts came rushing at him like an express train. Karen Palmer had once worked with him, a secretary in the huge engineering company to which he'd been contracted. She'd done everything to try to get him to sleep with her, or form a relationship with her, and he had known instinctively that it was his money and not his fatal charm which had attracted her.

'The twins are Karen's. And yours,' she added, just to make sure he got the picture.

He clenched his fists. He wasn't going to be conned by some fiery-headed madam, who was probably trying to tap into his wealth. Unless she was totally ignorant of the facts of life, she ought to know that to make someone pregnant you had to have sex with them – and he and Karen hadn't even come close to that sort of relationship.

'That's not possible. I don't know what cock-and-bull story Karen has fed you, but those babies have *nothing* to do with me.'

As if to reassure himself, he glanced down at the babies and the first touch of doubt feathered across his mind. There was no way the babies could be his, of course, but in that quick glance a strange feeling of familiarity had stirred deep in his gut. He shook his head slightly as if to clear the ridiculous thought away. He had never touched Karen Palmer, and if one of her babies had thick black hair and a look that tugged at his memory, then it was just a coincidence.

Despite his hell-raising life style, he hadn't really played fast and loose with women, always practising safe sex and letting them know that commitment wasn't on his agenda. There were plenty of woman who had the same blueprint, who wanted a career not a family, but who enjoyed male company and a short-term relationship.

'Karen said they were yours.'

Nicholas jerked his head up. The expression on the small upturned face was shocked and confused. He wondered what convoluted story she'd been fed and had obviously swallowed in one gulp.

'Karen said they were yours,' she insisted. 'She said if anything happened to her, you would take them under your wing.'

'Tell me,' Nicholas said, 'do you believe in the goddamn tooth fairy, too?'

She absorbed his insults like little daggers thudding into her thin frame. He could almost feel her pain. Her eyes rounded like saucers. They were a dead give-away. Huge green pools reflecting her emotions. For the first time he noticed the shadows under her eyes, the unconscious slump of her shoulders. She had almost reached the end of her endurance. Why? What part did she play in this fiasco?

Impatiently he waved his arms in the air, shocked when she stepped back. She looked apprehensive and afraid. Of him? Just as well she couldn't see into his mind.

Everything about her, her fragility, the proud lift of her chin, the fiery-red hair, threw him off balance. He drew in a quick breath. Surely she didn't expect to deposit two babies on his doorstep, then take off and leave him to cope?

He dropped his hands to his sides and thrust his chin out aggressively. 'Let's get one thing straight here. Karen and I at no stage had a relationship – not that she didn't make unmistakable overtures. Believe me, I am definitely *not* the father of her children.'

He stood back while she took his words on board, but she shook her head. 'She wouldn't have lied to me.'

For a moment he was speechless. *Of course*, she would have lied. Karen had made an art form of lying. She'd tried to use him and his wealth as a ticket to a luxurious lifestyle, and when it hadn't worked she'd veered off the track and come completely unstuck. Who she'd veered off the track with, he had no idea and even less interest, but she'd obviously dragged her sister into the mire to take over her responsibilities.

Where the hell was the main player in this event, anyway? Just like Karen to create havoc and expect someone else to clean up after her!

'She wouldn't have lied.' Green eyes targeted his near

black ones, holding his gaze. 'Not...' Her voice broke. 'Not when she was dying.'

The air hissed from his lungs like a deflated balloon. Oh, hell! Karen had tried to play him for a sucker, but now she was dead... He drew in a ragged breath as he remembered her tall blonde beauty. Despite his abhorrence when she'd tried to 'come on' to him, he would never have wished her any harm.

He tried to speak, but there was no sound. The green eyes were overflowing now, and he felt like Low Life personified. He was reaching out an arm to comfort her, when an ear-splitting shriek virtually shook the basket at his feet.

His heart beat accelerated almost to the point of cardiac arrest. He'd never heard anything like it. That experience was instantly repeated as the bawling twin set off a chain reaction and the other one began shrieking in unison. He looked towards his diminutive visitor for guidance and she put her face in her hands and sobbed.

chapter two

It was one of those rare occasions when he nearly panicked. But common-sense surfaced just in time. He had worked in some hell-holes over the years, quelled virtual mutinies and survived an earthquake. Quietening three howling individuals should be a piece of cake. Right?

Wrong!

The noise from the basket was deafening, while the sobs wrenched from the slender-framed girl standing in front of him were only a tad less devastating.

He picked up the basket and marched into the house. As he expected, Mother Goose followed. He swung the basket on to the table. It was a larger than normal baby basket, and heavy even for his superior strength.

'How in God's name did you manage to carry that basket?' he demanded turning to confront her.

Shock treatment seemed to work. She gulped and ran the back of her hand across her face in a childlike gesture.

'I carried the basket separately and then moved the babies one at a time from the car. I can't manage them both at once.' This confession seemed about to cause another avalanche of tears, but she clenched her fists and went towards the door.

'Where do you think you're going?' This time he did panic. He couldn't think of anything more daunting than being left with two babies. He glanced quickly at the two roaring, gummy mouths and winced. Boy! They should have been born with volume control.

'I left a bag of essentials beside the basket,' she said.

'You'll need that.'

He was beside her in seconds, breathing hell-fire and brimstone. 'Correction! *You'll* need it,' he said grimly. 'I've already told you that I'm *not* their father.'

'You don't know that,' she said. 'They're hungry. I need to make up their bottles.'

As she went out of the door, he leaned back against the table. Oh, he knew all right. He was no more those babies' father than he was a monkey's uncle, but convincing their keeper of that fact was proving to be almost a mission impossible.

'You could try picking them up,' she announced as she hurried back inside with a backpack slung over one shoulder. 'Where's the kitchen?'

Pick them up! Was she mad? He looked at his large hands. Hands that had done hard manual labour; hands that had manipulated intricate electrical equipment; hands that had stroked and caressed a woman's body. But, those hands sure as hell had never, ever held a baby.

She found the kitchen without his help and, as she clattered bottles and tins, he stood transfixed watching the little faces crumpled with distress. The baby with the thatch of black hair had stopped crying temporarily, but the little redhead was crimson in the face and becoming almost hysterical. Suddenly the hysteria stopped and the baby went limp.

Stark terror flooded Nicholas' system. Oh-my-God…the child had clearly lapsed into a coma! Maybe even… He grabbed the baby up into his arms. However, what he had mistaken for unconsciousness had been just the baby's way of regrouping for another screaming session, and as he thrust the baby against his shoulder another bloodcurdling shriek split his eardrums.

'Oh good. You've picked Sally up. She's the placid one.'

The blood was still rushing around in Nicholas' head, like the suds in a washing machine. '*Placid*!' he roared. 'She should be given an Academy Award.'

'She's hungry, Mr Best.'

What was it about this Miss Goody-Two-Shoes which made him feel like something one found under a rock? Mr Best…? *No one* called him Mr Best.

She thrust a bottle at him and without thinking he sat down and cradled the baby, before putting the bottle in her mouth. By the time that he realised what he was doing, she had taken the other baby and was following suit.

She gave him a nervous smile. 'This one's called Sam,' she said.

His heart lurched. His brother had been called Sam. Memories rushed back and with the expertise born of practice, he quickly banished them. He looked across at the pair sitting opposite him. The little boy was sucking lustily at his bottle and the love in the eyes of the woman holding him was obvious for anyone to see.

He glanced down at the little girl making short work of her feed. Karen had been blonde, but he supposed that if she had a sister with red hair, then she could have produced a child with red hair. Sam! Why call her child Sam, unless she was trying to reinforce the connection to him – and what on earth did she hope to gain by doing so?

'You'll need to burp her.' Auntie interrupted his thought pattern as she monitored his progress.

Auntie who? He had certainly never discussed her family with Karen, and he'd had no idea that she had a sister. 'What's your name?' he asked, gingerly removing the bottle from Sally's mouth and expecting all hell to break loose.

'Grace. Grace Palmer. I'm Karen's half-sister. We had the same father.'

'Had…? Your father's dead?'

'Yes. Karen's mother died when she was eight. A year later her father married my mother, and a year after that I was born. My parents were killed in a road accident. Karen and I only had each other and even so we weren't close.'

'Then why are you looking after her children? Is that why you want to get rid of them?'

She drew in an agonised breath. 'I don't *want* to get rid of them. I just can't cope on my own. I don't have the resources.'

'Financial resources?' His mouth twisted unpleasantly. She could well be just another leech after his wealth.

'Yes, and physical. Twins need a lot of care and they've been poor sleepers. I felt that I couldn't cope without help.'

'Surely Karen left some assets? Why else would she leave the babies in your care?'

As far as he was concerned, the whole story sounded very fishy. Karen had obviously lied to her sister about the twins' father, but what had she hoped to achieve? Once again his thoughts revolved in disarray. There was definitely something missing here…if he could just put his finger on it.

Grace bit her lip. 'Karen didn't have much money, and what little she had was eaten up in medical bills and buying the things we needed for the twins.'

Nicholas swallowed uncomfortably. 'What did she die from?'

'Meningitis. The twins were only a few weeks old.'

'How old are they now?'

It was a loaded question and she hesitated before answering.

She looked up at him defiantly, daring him to argue. 'Five months. They were a couple of weeks early.'

He sighed. Five months ago he'd been in Saudi Arabia.

It was a time of his life which he would have preferred to forget, but he knew that he never would. He glanced at the downy red head. The little girl looked up at him and burped loudly.

He put the bottle back in her mouth and looked over at Grace, who was patting the little boy on the back. He was as dark as his sister was fair.

'Whoever fathered that child was either Italian or a damned gypsy,' Nick said irritably.

She looked at him in astonishment. 'What about your hair? It's as black as coal. Except for...' Her eyes rested on the thick streak of silver running through his dark hair.

He glared at her. If appearance was the only criterion, then he supposed they could be his children. God forbid! He needed children like a hole in the head. Especially at this point in his life. Hell! At *any* point in his life. He was not fatherhood material and he never would be.

In any case, the world was full of dark, olive-skinned men. Take his entire family: his father, his brother Sam, even his Uncle Will – they'd all been branded with the family's black hair and eyes the colour of treacle. He glanced at the little boy again. Sam...? Dear God – the baby looked just like his brother Sam!

Nick drew in a deep breath, slowing the thoughts that reverberated like gunshots through his mind. That extraordinary sense of familiarity. If he'd allowed his thoughts to go down that track earlier, instead of banishing them as he always did when thoughts of Sam entered his mind, he'd have realised who the little boy looked like. Because he was the spitting image of Sam. Now the name came to take on a whole new meaning. Could...could they be Sam's children?

Desperately he cleared his mind of thoughts which he felt unable to deal with. The little girl had finished her bottle and gone off to sleep. She felt warm and soft in his arms, but he had a sudden urge to put her down. He and babies were incompatible and that was a fact.

'That damn basket is too small for two babies. You can't keep them in that.' Take charge of the situation. That was it. She'd been firing bullets at him since her surprise attack. Now he'd fire a few salvos of his own.

'They shared a large cot at…at my place. I just used the basket to transport them.'

'You were just going to dump them on my doorstep like unwanted baggage?' He gave her a furious look. How dare she come across like Mother Teresa? What she had planned was criminal.

'It wasn't like that.' She held the little boy close, setting the empty bottle on the floor by her chair. 'The last thing I wanted was to give them up, but I had to do what was best for them. I told you that I don't have the money to bring them up and you…'

'Oh, I've got plenty of money – and you've obviously done your homework. I've only recently bought this old farm, but you found out that I had taken up permanent residence here, didn't you? That takes care of the financial aspect and the roof over the twins' heads, of course. But, what about the moral issue? I could be a child molester for all you know.'

'But you're not.'

'How do you know?'

'Karen wouldn't have had a relationship with a child molester.'

He rose to his feet, hoisting Sally up on his shoulder. Her head flopped against his neck and he steeled himself against her baby softness.

'Believe me, given enough financial inducement, Karen would have got together with Jack the Ripper!'

Grace shot out of her chair giving Sam the hiccups. 'That's a rotten thing to say,' she protested.

How could she tell him that she had agonised over her decision? Karen had said he was a devil, but when questioned she hadn't really come up with any diabolical facts.

Grace knew that he didn't have a criminal record. She didn't exactly have friends in high places, but Karen's fund of still-besotted ex-boyfriends had yielded a high-ranking police officer who'd run a check on Nicholas Best. 'Clean as the proverbial whistle,' he'd told Grace with something suspiciously like regret.

'Rotten or not, you still took a risk. In fact, how do you know that you're safe in my house?' He leered at her. 'I have a reputation for eating and spitting out little innocents like you.' He took a step towards her and she backed away.

'You wouldn't. That's all newspaper talk. The media make things up.' She stepped back towards him, her chin up high. 'I'm not in the least afraid of you. You're not as bad as you're painted.'

He'd give her ten out of ten for nerve. She clearly wasn't going to be intimidated. His undeserved reputation *was* all paper talk, although he'd never done anything to counteract the wild stories which occasionally appeared in the press. But he was surprised that she was astute enough to judge them for the fiction that they were. She couldn't be sure of her facts unless… The penny dropped with a loud clang.

'You had me investigated didn't you?'

'That's ridiculous…' she began.

'Oh spare me the phoney indignation,' he said keeping a rein on his temper with difficulty. 'What did they tell you? Everything but my shoe size…? But then, I can't buy my shoes in a regular store. I get them made. Did they tell you that? Did they tell you that it's not only my feet which are outsize? Would you like the actual measurement?'

'No!' Her face was ablaze. He'd rattled her cage this time. 'You're disgusting,' she retorted.

Yep! She was rattled all right. Good! She might go and take the blasted babies with her. The thought didn't give him any satisfaction. He was no knight in shining armour, but he couldn't turn them out into the street.

As if to reinforce his decision, Sally nestled closer to his neck and he felt his stomach turn to mush. He forced himself to think of Karen and her manipulative ways as he tried to harden his heart.

He'd be doing some investigating himself, but in the meantime he was stuck with the problem of Mummy Bear and her two babies. Why couldn't they live in Goldilocks's house?

'You must have lived somewhere,' he said. 'Why can't you take the babies back with you and I'll provide financial support? For the time being,' he amended hastily. No sense in handing it to her on a platter.

'I don't have a house,' she said. 'I was staying with friends.'

'You said they slept in a cot at your place.' She was being evasive and he smelt a rat.

'I meant where I was living. It isn't my house. I can't go on living there. The home that my parents left to Karen and myself had to be sold.'

'You must have some financial backing.' Karen had earned big money in her secretarial position and grudgingly he had to admit that she had been good at her job.

She shook her head. 'I know what you're thinking. Karen did have the capacity to earn good money, but once she became pregnant that was no longer possible. She was so sick during her pregnancy that she was hospitalised for a lot of the time and she had no health insurance. We paid for private care and it cost a fortune.'

That figured. No public hospital for Karen. The 'we paid' wasn't lost on Nicholas, either.

'If you add her time in intensive care before she died and the special care the twins needed at birth, you'll understand how thousands of dollars were swallowed up.'

He didn't doubt that she was telling the truth, but there was something he couldn't quite put his finger on. Something that she wasn't telling him.

Unfortunately, any thought of sending her packing with a large cheque had just been blown out of the water. Sally breathed out, blowing bubbles against his neck. He sighed heavily as he felt the noose tightening.

'The first problem is to find somewhere for these two to sleep,' he said.

She sagged with relief. 'Then you'll let them stay? You'll look after them?'

'Yes, I'll let them stay – and no, *you'll* look after them.' He derived a nasty satisfaction from the shattered look on her face.

'But, that means…I'll have to stay here. In your house.'

'That's exactly what it means. You've put your head in the lion's mouth, Grace, and if I find out that you've been lying, I'll damn well bite it off.'

chapter three

He made things happen, she couldn't deny that. Grace sat in a huge leather chair and looked at the sleeping twins. They were lying on a thick rug spread on the Persian carpet. Their cots would arrive later in the day, along with all the other baby paraphernalia that Nicholas had ordered.

He entered the room holding a mobile phone to his ear. His expressive face said it all. He wasn't happy, and when his mouth twisted in anger she unconsciously shrank back into the soft cushions.

'I don't pay you to make excuses,' he roared into the phone. 'I pay for progress and if you don't make some soon, you'll be warming a spot in the dole queue.'

Grace winced. Obviously, anyone who didn't shape-up got shipped-out. She thought of her own tenuous predicament. She let her breath ease out slowly. He wouldn't get rid of her because, like it or not, he needed her.

Unless he decided to throw them all out, but he'd had the opportunity to do that and he hadn't acted on it. Perhaps even the devil had a soft side?

'For God's sake, stop burrowing into that chair like a rabbit looking for refuge.' He hurled the phone on to a nearby table and gave her a look that would have sizzled bacon.

So much for the soft side! Grace told herself grimly, standing up and confronting him. 'Don't take your business problems out on me, Mr Best. I'm sure that you'd get more out of your staff by using encouragement instead of brow-beating them.'

His jaw dropped open. 'Do you? And I suppose you know all about running a profitable business, so that the staff in question still have a job? Believe me, Miss Perfection, every one of my employees needs to pull their weight, and I haven't got time to wipe their bottoms for them.'

She shuddered. He was disgusting. 'I still think, Mr Best, that the way you spoke to that man was horrible.'

'Woman,' he corrected and, when he saw her shocked look, he gave her a nasty smile and repeated, 'The recipient of my ill humour was a woman.'

He really was a devil. And it seemed as though he could read her thoughts when he added, 'For God's sake stop calling me Mr Best. My name is Nicholas and I'm always called Nick.'

What else, she thought. Nick was the devil himself – and it looked as if his namesake was running true to form.

He ran his eyes over her small form and she felt as if they'd left scorch marks where they paused. She felt uneasy. He couldn't possibly fancy her. She wasn't his type.

His words came as a complete surprise. 'You'll need more than a pair of jeans and a T-shirt while you're here. I suppose I'd better buy you some clothes.'

She felt her cheeks blazing. 'You'll do no such thing. I have a suitcase full of clothes in the car.'

His eyes narrowed. 'You were going to leave the babies and do a bunk. Why bring clothes?'

'I…' she hesitated. 'I was going to stay around for a while. Not here,' she added hastily. 'I thought that if I stayed in town, I could keep an eye on things.'

'On me, you mean. Lady, you slay me. What would you have done if you wanted the babies back? Kidnapped them?'

'I don't know. I hadn't thought it through.'

'Seems to me you don't think *anything* through.'

Her shoulders slumped. He was right of course. She'd made decisions without giving a thought to the result. She'd let her heart and her emotions guide her through life and she'd ended by being caught up in a whirlpool of confusion. Grace realised that the emotional upheaval of the last few months – the lack of money, which in its turn had led to a lack of good food and, most of all, the absence of a family to support her – had all contributed to impulsive and bad decisions.

No one could accuse Nick of indecision. Within a few hours, a large delivery truck pulled up outside the farm-house and two men began unloading the items which he'd ordered. They almost fell over each other to do his bidding and Grace wondered what incentives he had offered to get such preferential treatment.

She watched him as he cleared the room to be used as a nursery and helped to install the furniture. His strength more than matched that of the burly delivery men and she felt a strange feeling deep within her. It was a blend of emotions that made her head spin.

His size and strength gave her a feeling of security and safety, which was ridiculous when she thought of her tenuous position and the fact that she knew so little about him. When she looked at him, she felt that no one and nothing could hurt her. But that feeling was immediately followed by a searing twinge of fear. Physically, he would probably never harm her, but a sudden premonition of the emotional damage he could possibly inflict left her feeling terrified.

Instinctively, she knew that the emotional trauma she dreaded wasn't just confined to the future of the twins. There was something about Nicholas Best that reached an unawakened part of her psyche which had lain dormant for too long.

She was still standing in the room, stunned by her thoughts and feelings, when Nick arrived back from paying the men and seeing them on their way.

'The new furniture makes the room look shabby,' he said, frowning at the faded wallpaper and the dingy curtains. 'This whole farmhouse is going to be renovated, but first I have to get the factory up and running.'

'Factory?' Grace's voice faltered as she struggled to get her thoughts back on track. It was a moment or two before she realised that, while she would be doing her best to bring up the twins, she would be living in the midst of renovations. Add to that the prospect of living with a man possessed with the establishment of a new venture, and she was sure that she had the perfect recipe for a nervous breakdown.

'Yes, factory.'

Grace heard the thrum of satisfaction in his deep voice. The fulfilment of a dream? Only he would know and he wasn't likely to share his dreams with her. She wondered if he had shared them with Karen. She doubted it. He seemed very self-sufficient.

He took her arm and propelled her into the next room. 'Your room,' he said subjecting the wallpaper to another searing look. 'We've got to get rid of this awful paper.'

Grace rather liked it. She suspected that the dingy yellow had originally been cream, and the flower pattern had faded to a dusky rose. It was outdated and a total misfit in the modern world. Like her, Grace thought. Her ideals and standards had been the target of ridicule more than once.

Karen's tinkle of laughter surfaced in her mind. 'Oh darling!' she'd said. 'Come and live in the real world.'

Grace shook her head to clear her mind. She was living

in the real world now with a ready-made family – and a man who was going to see that she danced to his tune. Clenching her fists, Grace was determined to be no man's puppet. If he tried to bully her, Nick was going to find that under her slight frame there was pure, tempered steel.

Nick saw her clench her fists. That was a battle stance if ever he'd seen one. He hastened to nullify the impending storm. 'I know it's not much of a bedroom,' he said. 'I'd rip the wallpaper off myself, but I'm too involved in establishing a new business.'

He could almost feel the tension ooze from her body. She glanced at the wallpaper with a smile.

'The wallpaper's fine,' she said.

She liked it? He almost threw up. It was sickly sweet. It wasn't even pristine sickly sweet. How could she even tolerate it?

Nick was no psychologist, but her taste in wallpaper gave him a small window into her soul and he didn't like what he saw. Being stuck with twins was bad enough, but to have to share his house with Miss Squeaky Clean was not likely to enhance his comfort zone.

It was late afternoon when he left for the factory. It nestled on a hill in the hinterland of Queensland's Sunshine Coast. As he guided his big four-wheel drive vehicle along the winding road, he looked around at the beautiful countryside. Dairy herds dotted the green rolling hills and flowering native trees added splashes of red, yellow and white.

He passed pineapple farms on his way, and large plantations with pawpaw, custard apples and exotic fruits. It was a prosperous and productive area. The words were music to his ears. His factory would prosper and if his staff got their act together, in a short time they would be productive.

He stopped the car in front of the round concrete building. Using an abandoned reservoir had presented some problems. Having the windows cut had been murder, but he liked the idea. He liked it a lot. He grinned. The environmentalists were very active in the area and they couldn't accuse him of not recycling.

He swung open the heavy door. It was like a beehive inside. People were moving around setting up machinery and unpacking crates.

'Oy! He's here. Old Nick.'

Nick heard the whispered warning and watched the domino effect with interest. One by one they laid down their tools and looked at him. The cheerful atmosphere was doused in gloom.

He felt about as welcome as bubonic plague, but that was immaterial. At least they knew who was boss and who filled their pay packet at the end of each week.

'Carry on,' he said. They fell over each other to resume their respective tasks and if the word browbeaten sprang to mind, he quickly disposed of it. What would Grace know about running a business? She couldn't even manage to bring up two babies without pushing the panic button.

He strode into his office. It doubled as a design room at the moment and he would be spending most of his time here, designing the components needed in the electrical engineering industry. It was a far cry from the work he'd done all over the world, but he was highly skilled technically and he was tired of risking life and limb in some of the world's hot spots.

He sank into the plush office chair and massaged the back of his neck. His fingers dipped into the depression left by the bullet. It had been a bullet with his name on it. He knew that for certain. Just as well that the terrorist had been over-confident and under-skilled. His hand fell down by his side. The whole incident still gave him the creeps.

Hours later, he stood up with a sense of accomplishment. His computer system was now up and running and he could see some real progress at last. He glanced at his watch. Ten o'clock. He looked through the glass window to the factory floor. Everyone had left of course. They all had commitments and time schedules. He grimaced. He couldn't live like that. No sir!

He quashed the uneasy feeling that if the twins were Sam's, he already had a commitment whether he wanted it or not. There was no point in arguing that he wasn't responsible for Sam's indiscretions or shortcomings.

He turned from the window with a gut wrenching sigh. Hadn't he always picked up after Sam? He'd spent a lifetime keeping him out of trouble, despite the fact that it was Sam who had been the preferred child. Sam who'd had the unquestioning devotion of parents, both of whom had ignored Nick almost to the point of rejection.

Nick left his office snapping off the light switch. He paused for a moment. In the end he had failed. He had let Sam down and now Sam was dead. Guilt flooded his system and he relegated it to the background, where he normally fought to keep it. Nothing that he did now would bring Sam back. A picture of two little babies, one heartbreakingly like his brother, suddenly flashed into his mind. He took a deep breath and headed towards the door.

He needed to keep a level head and behave rationally. Making decisions based on a deep, ingrained sense of guilt wouldn't help anyone, least of all two little babies who had practically nothing going for them. He thought of Grace, fiercely protective and battling against the odds. She'd even been prepared to give the babies up although, when it came to the crunch, she hadn't succeeded. Perhaps they did have someone to fight their battles after all.

Activating the alarm system, he left the factory, slamming the door on both his workplace and his grim thoughts at the same time.

Half an hour later, the Range Rover ground to a halt in the barn which he used as a garage. He reached across the seat and retrieved the pizza that he had picked up on the way home. Home? Yeah! It was beginning to feel a bit like home. He glanced at the house. It was lit up like a power station. The front door opened and Grace stood under the porch light.

He grinned. Her head looked as if it was on fire. Boy – did she have red hair! It was thick and curly, but too damned short. He tried to picture it flowing around her shoulders or piled up on top of her head. Whoa! He pulled his thoughts into line. He didn't give a damn how she wore her hair, and there was no need for her to stand waiting for him like the proverbial little woman, either.

'Why aren't you in bed?' he barked when he reached the doorway.

'And Hello to you, too,' she said turning on her heel and marching back into the house.

'I meant that you didn't have to wait up,' he said, trying to salvage household harmony. He watched her rigid back as he followed her into the kitchen and placed the pizza box on the table. If there was one thing he was learning and learning quickly, it was that this lady wasn't going to stand for any… The word 'browbeating' flashed into his mind again and he suppressed a grin.

'The twins have to be fed around ten o'clock, so there isn't much point in going to bed before then.'

He retrieved a knife from the cutlery drawer, swearing as it stuck when he tried to close it. 'This kitchen is the pits,' he growled, cutting a large wedge of pizza and placing it on a plate in front of her, before glancing at his watch. 'It's after ten-thirty,' he pointed out.

'They can't tell the time,' she said. 'I'll wake them in a minute.'

He choked on his pizza. 'Wake them? Why would you do that?'

'Because I'd rather feed them now, than at two o'clock in the morning.'

His eyes glazed over. Two o'clock in the morning! He looked at her. 'Wake them,' he said.

She was pushing the pizza around on her plate. 'I'm not really hungry,' she told him. 'I had tea earlier.' She hesitated. 'I cooked some for you too.'

'There's no need to do that,' he said. Next she'd be putting his slippers in front of the fire, except that he'd never owned a pair in his life.

'You have to eat,' she pointed out.

'I do,' he said indicating the pizza.

'You can't eat pizza every night,' she said.

She shimmered with disapproval. He enjoyed enlightening her. 'Oh, not every night. I alternate with fried chicken, spare ribs and fish and chips.'

'That's really bad for your heart,' she said.

'Ah, Grace, you're missing the point. I don't have a heart. If I had a dollar for the number of times I've been called a heartless bastard, I'd be as rich as Croesus.'

She filled and warmed the feeding bottles, while he demolished her slice of pizza. He must have been really hungry. Her eyes took in the huge frame sprawled in the flimsy kitchen chair. It wouldn't only be his shoes which he had tailor made. He had long legs and very broad shoulders. She found herself staring at the silver streak in his thick black hair, which gave him such an unusual, slightly devilish appearance. But just then Sally began to whimper and Grace jumped.

'Thank Goodness for that.' Nick commented. 'I thought you'd gone into suspended animation. Either that or I'd acquired head lice.'

'Ugh! What a thing to say. I was only wondering why a lock of your hair should have turned a sort of silvery colour…?'

He stood up, seeming to tower over her despite the fact that she was quite tall. It wasn't so much his height which made her feel somewhat overwhelmed, but the strength of his personality which seemed to almost come out and grab her. She shook her head in an effort to dispel such fanciful thoughts.

'I seem destined to be different,' he said with a trace of cynicism. 'I've been told that I cut a swathe through life, leaving a trail of devastation behind me.'

'You don't.' Despite the fears he subconsciously aroused, Grace didn't believe he was half as bad as he was painting himself.

He shrugged. 'Maybe not, but my mother seemed to think so.'

There was a bitter note to his voice and Grace felt a chill run down her spine. A mother who could make such an accusation would have little feeling for her son's self-esteem.

Sally's piercing cry put an end to the conversation and Grace rushed in to the bedroom to lift the little girl from the cot. She took her out into the living room and put her on a thick rug on the floor, propping the bottle in her mouth with a small pillow. She wasn't happy about leaving her there, but she had to retrieve Sam who had joined in the chorus.

By the time she went back into the living room with Sam and his bottle, Nick had Sally in his arms and the bottle in her mouth.

Grace gave him a grateful smile. 'Thanks.'

'How do you usually feed them?' Nick cast a dark look at the floor. 'Surely a rug and a pillow make a poor substitute for a mother's arms?'

Grace hid her surprise. She hadn't expected him to be so sensitive. 'I only resort to those measures when there's no one to help me.'

He gave her a black look. 'I was here.'

'Yes, but…'

He raised one eyebrow daring her to finish the sentence.

'You don't really want them… us… here. I'm just trying not to disrupt your life too drastically.'

He threw back his head and laughed, causing Sally to lose her hold on the bottle. Her little face crumpled and Nick hastily shoved the bottle back into her mouth.

'Excuse me,' he said. 'You dump a basket of babies on my porch, prepare to clear off and you don't want to disrupt my life…?'

'I told you. I was desperate.'

'Why?'

'I had nowhere to go. I couldn't expect friends to house me any longer.'

He sat Sally up and rubbed her back. Grace bit back a smile. He wasn't even aware of how many baby skills he'd acquired in a few short hours.

'So when did you become involved with Karen and her pregnancy? And if she was so sure that I was the father, why didn't she contact me right from the word go?'

Grace settled Sam in her lap and gave him his bottle. 'She contacted me when she was too ill to work and needed someone to look after her. When I asked her about the babies' father, she said that he was working in Saudi Arabia.'

Sally burped loudly and Nick absently shoved the bottle

back in her mouth. He did a rough calculation, working out the time when Karen would have been pregnant. 'I was in Saudi Arabia then,' he admitted. And Sam had also been there at the same time. So, if Sam really *was* the twins' father, in a way Karen hadn't exactly been telling a lie.

He glanced down at Sally. She'd gone to sleep on her bottle. He ran a finger over her silky hair.

'Besides…' Grace said.

He took the bottle out of Sally's mouth and hoisted her on to his shoulder, totally unaware of how small she looked against the breadth of his body.

'Besides what?' Nick prompted.

Grace shrugged her shoulders, almost making baby Sam lose his grip on the bottle. 'She said that the father of her babies wouldn't want anything to do with them. She said that he told her to take precautions to avoid getting pregnant.'

He hesitated. It sounded like Sam. Unfortunately, the sparks which those green eyes were hurling in his direction, clearly indicated that Grace believed he was the culprit. He thought about telling her that he suspected his brother was the twins' father, but something held him back.

It was, after all, only a suspicion and at this stage he wanted to remain in charge of the situation, even if it meant that Saint Grace was ready to have his guts for garters.

'So you just upped and left your job and came to the rescue.' Nick knew he sounded a little sceptical, but something about Grace bothered him. She seemed so unworldly and trusting. She shouldn't trust him. She knew nothing about him. Or, not very much, he corrected himself, his mouth twisting in a wry grin as he recalled the fact that she'd had him investigated.

'I was between jobs,' Grace said.

It was a very quick reply – almost too quick. Nick felt

that there was a lot she wasn't revealing. Although Sam's edict about avoiding pregnancy was vintage Sam, he did have a point. Someone of Karen's experience and frankly loose morals would have at least been on the Pill. So, how did she get pregnant? If she'd hoped to trap Sam into marriage, it only went to show that she didn't know Sam very well.

'Frankly, I wouldn't have thought Karen was likely to get pregnant.' Nick chose his words carefully, cautiously picking his way through the minefield of deception.

'She certainly didn't intend to,' Grace said. 'She told me that she was taking the Pill, but a bout of food poisoning rendered it ineffective. I think her pregnancy was a shock to her. I'm sure that she would have been in denial for a long time.'

Probably too long for abortion to be a possibility, Nick realised, drawing in a deep breath. Maybe he was misjudging her? Whatever the reason for Karen going through with her pregnancy and keeping the babies, he was glad that she did. If they were Sam's babies, then it meant that a small part of the brother he had loved still existed.

His thoughts flew off at a tangent as he thought about that love. Strange under the circumstances. The fact that his own father had rejected him, and his mother had distanced herself from him – while they both showered the love they denied Nick on his younger brother – should have fostered hate not love. Starved of someone to care for, Nick had nurtured his young brother, finding some consolation in the almost hero worship response that Sam had directed towards him.

With hindsight, he now realised that he shouldn't have fought Sam's battles for him or overprotected him. When faced with the inevitable adversities that life throws in one's path, Sam hadn't been able to cope and as he grew to adulthood, Nick hadn't been there to remove the obstacles.

Grace thought about the questions Nick had asked and her evasive answers. She had no intention of baring her soul to Nicholas Best.

She had made sacrifices for her sister and looked after her during her pregnancy and her final illness. She stifled a sigh. She knew that Karen had accepted everything done for her as her right and rarely, except at the end of her life, had she expressed any gratitude.

Memories of her sister's death flooded into her mind and Grace banished them quickly. She hadn't wanted or needed gratitude, because she had loved Karen unconditionally and now she would direct that love to her sister's children.

Sam had finished his bottle and Grace sat him up, rubbing his back. He squirmed for a while and then obligingly burped.

'What now?' Nick said, rising to his feet with Sally still draped on his shoulder.

'We… I…put them to bed.' Grace stood up heaving Sam on to her shoulder. He was getting heavy so she must be doing something right.

'*We* put them to bed,' Nick said. 'You said yourself that you couldn't manage them both at once.'

He led the way into the makeshift nursery and watched as Grace dropped a kiss on Sam's head, before putting him in his cot.

He lowered Sally from his shoulder, paused for a moment, and then held her out for Grace to kiss her head. She hid a smile as she took the baby and put her in the other cot. It was expecting a bit much for him to kiss the babies, especially as he always looked as if he half-expected them to self-destruct in his arms.

Grace punched her pillow for the umpteenth time. It had been quite a day and she felt exhausted, but she couldn't sleep. It wasn't the lumpy bed. After the hard, narrow bed she'd been used to, a double bed with lumps was still a luxury.

She sighed. Once again she'd made a hasty decision – but at least involving Nick had been her own decision. Putting her life on hold to bring up her sister's babies hadn't been so much her decision, as a case of sheer necessity.

There hadn't been anyone else and, despite the fact that she'd loved her sister, they had never been close. Even so, there was no way that she could have refused to help her. And now... now the twins were entwined in her heart, her life. In fact, they *were* her life. She realised that she could never have left them on Nick's doorstep and walked away.

She could hear the creak of the bed in the next room. Nick's room. His bed sounded about the same vintage as hers. For a man who was supposed to be wealthy, his home and its contents, if you discounted the leather chairs and the Persian rugs, were downright tatty. Not that she cared about that. Material possessions had never meant a lot to Grace, which was just as well considering what she had done with the little wealth she'd once possessed.

chapter four

Nick shot up in bed, clouting his head on the old-fashioned bed-head. Something had woken him. The air hissed out of his lungs as he recognised a baby's cry. It was Sally. He knew without checking. That little madam had eardrum torture down to a fine art.

He relaxed back against the pillows, noting with disgust that his large feet hung over the end of the bed. He really had to do something to make life more liveable. This old house needed gutting and renovating, while most of the furniture must have come out of the ark. Possessions had never meant a great deal to him, although he'd collected a few bits and pieces during his travels.

He felt his body tense again. Sally was still crying. Where the hell was Grace? His feet hit the floor and he grabbed an old towelling robe. It barely covered the essentials, but that was the least of his worries.

He marched into the nursery shaking his head as he picked Sally up. He'd slept through a multitude of weird noises in foreign countries, including gunfire, and here he was at six o'clock in the morning instantly awake at the sound of a baby's cry.

Sally smiled a gummy smile, her bout of crying turned off like a tap. Nick stood totally nonplussed. Her little mouth opened wider. Terrified that she was about to bellow again Nick flashed her a grin that would have done a tooth-paste advertisement proud.

Grace. Where on earth was she? He stumbled into her room and almost dropped Sally. Grace lay on the bed in a deep sleep, her arm flung above her head. Rumpled red curls encircled her head like a fiery halo. Her plain white cotton night-dress had ridden up above her thighs, displaying a gorgeous pair of legs.

Forget the legs, Best! Nick told himself firmly. She looked about sixteen and he was no cradle snatcher. His eyes had other ideas as they travelled further, noting the chaste cotton panties under the nightie. His eyes almost started from their sockets. This was Karen's sister?

He dragged some air into his lungs. Sally was beginning to squirm and she was Grace's problem not his. He hitched Sally on to his hip and stretched out a hand to shake Grace awake. She turned her face towards him, still asleep, and it was then that he saw the dark circles under her eyes. Oh Lord! He turned away leaving her to rest.

'Come on, Sally. It looks like it's just you and me.' There were bottles made up in the fridge. He had seen them when he'd had a late snack.

He stretched out a hand to open the fridge door and his nose twitched. Phew! Young Sally smelled to high heaven. She couldn't have…?

Her little face screwed up in disgust and he didn't blame her. But change her? He set his agile mind to the problem. He'd coped with worse events than changing a baby. On one occasion he'd helped to amputate a man's leg. He shuddered as he remembered once finding a body. And it hadn't been a fresh body, either. So changing a dirty nappy ought to be easy.

He'd made a decision to let Grace sleep, so he took Sally back to the nursery and put her on the changing table. After undoing what seemed like a million clips on her sleep suit, he exposed the nappy. It looked innocent enough. He wasn't terribly *au fait* where nappies were concerned, but he was pretty sure that it was the disposable kind. He let out a relieved breath. After making short work of the adhesive tapes he whipped the nappy off. Oh hell! A string of harsher expletives followed in quick succession. He grabbed a moist tissue and started to clean her up. His stomach did a series of loop the loops.

'Grace!' His bellow would have woken the dead. She hit the floor running and took in the scene in the nursery at a glance. He waited until she had a hand on Sally and then he covered his mouth and ran.

Ten minutes later Grace stood in the kitchen doorway holding Sally in her arms. Nick was sitting at the table with his head in his hands. He glanced at Sally as if she were an unexploded bomb.

'It's OK I've washed and changed her,' Grace told him. 'It gets easier after the first time.'

'Read my lips,' Nick said. 'That was positively the *last time* that I ever change a nappy!'

'If you give me half an hour to feed the babies, I'll cook you some breakfast.'

Nick shuddered. He doubted that he'd ever eat again. 'I have to go to the factory,' he said. 'I'll pick up something on the way.'

'Not pizza.' Grace looked aghast.

'No, doughnuts.'

'That's worse,' Grace said.

'Nothing…' Nick shuddered and started again. 'Nothing could be worse than the start I've had to the day. Now, I'm going to shower and leave for the factory.' He stood up and left the room.

Grace watched as he walked out. Her breathing suddenly became difficult. She must have developed an allergy. Yeah sure! It was six foot three and had long legs, barely covered by a disreputable old towelling robe. And what about the broad chest covered in silky black curls, revealed by loosely-tied robe…?

Grace's blood almost boiled. She took herself severely in hand. How did she know his chest hair was silky? It was probably like straw. You could easily find out, the little gremlin in her head suggested. She sat down suddenly and Sally set up a protest.

Automatically, Grace warmed Sally's bottle and as she fed her she tried to get her renegade thoughts under control. She didn't give a hoot about Nick's chest hair, or what it would feel like to have those huge arms around her, and to be kissed by those gorgeous lips.

Her head drooped as she groaned out loud. Where were these unfamiliar thoughts coming from? Nick Best had made 'been there – and done that' an art form, and he would never have done any of it with someone like her. And he never would, she added for good measure.

Nick decided to give the doughnuts a miss. Not that he believed all that rubbish about cholesterol, but he doubted his stomach would ever be fit to receive food again. Unfortunately his retentive memory kept replaying the incident. He shivered. He'd had a close shave, he acknowledged. In just one day, that little redhead had begun to make inroads into his hard-bitten character.

He nodded his head as he guided the Range Rover around the curving roads. No more, he decided. They could share his roof until he found out just whose kids they were – and then he would make some harsh decisions. He'd have to harden his heart against Mummy redhead too. Dark circles. He couldn't believe he'd let her fragility get to him like that. She was about as fragile as a female tiger with cubs.

He entered his premises with a sense of satisfaction. It

was going to be a great enterprise. He knew he had the skills to design and produce innovative electrical components, and he also liked the idea of providing employment for other people.

The office chair creaked in protest as he leaned his considerable weight back in it and picked up the envelope on his desk. It had probably been there yesterday, but he'd been too involved in setting up his computer to read any correspondence.

His mouth dropped open. One person wasn't interested in his effort to provide employment. It was a letter of resignation from the woman he had bawled out. 'Browbeaten'. Grace's words came back to haunt him. He hadn't really browbeaten the woman. Had he?

His fingers drummed on the desk as he recalled the phone conversation. Maybe he had been a tad impatient, but it wasn't every day he received a basket of babies and a red-headed virago attached to them.

By lunchtime, he'd made the necessary apology, ripped up the woman's resignation, decided his stomach had recovered and, as he ate some salad sandwiches, he wondered if he'd also lost his marbles. Nick Best wasn't big on apologies, but he liked to think he was fair. As he bit into a sandwich, he made one promise to himself. He definitely wasn't telling the fairy godmother what he'd done.

The pumpkin soup bubbled on the stove, and the 'bake at home rolls' turned golden brown in the oven. She'd probably have to eat it all herself, Grace thought. She'd found the pumpkin in the back yard and the rolls in the freezer, but there was little else left in the way of food except staples like cereal, milk, butter and bread. Even so, she'd managed to conjure up a decent meal. A wry smile twisted her mouth. Wasn't that her speciality, making a meal out of nothing?

She hadn't lied to Nick when she'd said that she'd lived with friends. But she had been responsible for her food and the formula for the babies. Her friends were not well off and even if they'd wanted to help her financially, they couldn't have done so. Despite the hardship, she had denied the babies nothing, giving them the special expensive formula which the clinic had said was necessary and making sure they were clean and comfortable at all times.

Until she had taken over the care of Sally and Sam, she'd had no idea how many small but expensive items were required during the process of bringing up a baby. And of course, in her case, the requirements had been doubled.

She stood back from the stove, placing a hand on her hip and immediately becoming conscious of the bones which she could feel under her clothing. Her duty towards the twins had not been without sacrifice and she knew that she had neglected her own health. She remembered the sudden feelings of panic that she could no longer cope, which had led to her decision to leave the babies with their father, and realised again that the downturn in her physical health had contributed in no small way to her rash decision.

She felt strung out and uncertain that she was doing the right thing, but her instincts told her that Nick would watch out for the babies. Even if they weren't his? The thought was immediately quashed. They were his. Karen had been emphatic about that. And even if he didn't want to acknowledge them, he would hardly have let them stay if he had any doubts.

She heard the Rover pull up in the barn and just managed to stop herself from opening the front door. He wasn't as late tonight, but then he'd left for the factory before seven that morning.

'Something smells good,' Nick said as he came into the kitchen. He clamped down hard on the memory of the morning's incident, which his mind seemed hell bent on replaying. He glanced cautiously around. The twins sat in a twin pram which he'd bought with all the other necessities. They were holding hands and he felt a strange sensation hit him amidships.

He looked away and cleared his throat. 'I decided to give the pizza a miss.'

'Oh! Fried chicken tonight is it?' Grace gave him a sweet smile as she shoved the knife in.

He looked hopefully towards the steam rising from the stove. 'Soup?'

'Pumpkin. But, I've taken to heart the comments you made about not cooking for you.'

He grinned like a little boy and Grace felt her insides do hula-hoops.

'That's a pity,' he said. 'I love pumpkin soup.'

He wasn't kidding, Grace thought, as he polished off his third bowl of soup. 'Did you have any lunch?' she asked.

He paused. 'Salad sandwiches. Don't go getting any ideas,' he said when he saw the small look of triumph on her face. 'I just ate what the rest of the staff were eating.'

'They must have more respect for their stomachs than you have.' Grace said. 'While we're on the subject of food, do you think you could do some shopping?'

'Shopping?'

By the look on his face, she might as well have spoken in a foreign language. 'Yes. Shopping. You know. You do it at the supermarket. You get a trolley and you fill it from the shelves.'

He stood up and came close, bending over her eyeball to eyeball. 'No,' he said. '*You* get a trolley and *you* fill it from the shelves. I go to the take-away outlet.'

'You enjoyed the pumpkin soup,' she pointed out. 'Three bowls of it.'

'You don't fight fair,' he said.

'I'm at a disadvantage.'

He straightened up. 'You shop. I'll pay.'

Grace squirmed uncomfortably. Feeding Nick would be like feeding the multitudes. She'd have to accept money from him. Her own small income wouldn't go anywhere.

'What's the problem?' he said, noting her discomfort.

'I'm not your responsibility. Only the twins.'

'Why let a little thing like that bother you? And…' he gave her a caustic look, 'I'm not convinced they belong to me. I'm just allowing for the possibility. Temporarily.'

A shiver passed over Grace's slight frame. What if Karen *had* lied? What if they weren't Nick's children? Sometimes it all became too complicated, too much to cope with. If Nick proved that they weren't his babies – then where would she be? Out on the street! She thought of the two beautiful babies and was unable to prevent weak tears from running down her cheeks.

Alarm bells started ringing as soon as Nick saw the tears tracking down her face. Jeez! He'd only said that he wouldn't go shopping. No, you didn't, his conscience shouted at him. You said the babies didn't belong to you – and that word 'temporarily' didn't go over too well, either. It made her feel insecure.

His own insecurities were buried in the past, but the scars they'd left were still there, easily opened again if he didn't keep them protected. He hauled her into his arms.

'Don't cry,' he said roughly. 'Two bawling babies is about as much as I can cope with. Besides, you don't eat much.'

She raised her swimming eyes and started to laugh. His head spun. She was beautiful. Such a fresh, pure beauty.

Like an appetiser to a jaded palate. He'd kissed her before he realised it. She tasted so sweet. He stifled a groan and all the warnings his brain was sending out went unheeded.

She felt like thistledown in his arms, but no thistledown had ever packed such a punch. He felt his body respond and he pulled her closer. She was as close as a second skin and her shocked reaction reverberated throughout his body as well.

He let her go at once, steadying her when she would have fallen. Her eyes were like saucers and she ran from the room. He sank down on to the chair, cursing himself for the fool that he was.

He didn't know much about Grace Palmer, but she sure as hell wasn't too clued-up about the male anatomy. As soon as she'd sensed his arousal, she'd practically had a seizure. Maybe it was because of those fool comments he'd made about his size.

No. It was more than that. She had been terrified! He shook his head. She was so childlike. He thought about the sweet curves of her breasts when he'd pressed her tightly against him. Her lips, soft and eager for a split second. No, she wasn't a child.

He ran an agitated hand through his hair. He had really messed up, big time. She was probably packing or calling the cavalry by now! No, she wouldn't be doing anything. After all, she had nowhere to go. Oh, that made him feel *really* good, he told himself grimly. He'd given her a little bit of security – and then practically eaten her alive. Well done! Good one, Best! Now, you'd better try and get yourself out of this predicament. If you can.

Grace sank down on to her bed. He'd only been trying to comfort her, but then everything changed. She chewed on her bottom lip. Had she sent out the wrong signals? Or was he just a man who turned situations to his own advantage? Her cheeks warmed as she thought of his reaction while holding her. It had come as a shock. She wasn't used to having that effect on men. But then, unlike Karen, she hadn't had all that much to do with men. Thoughts whirled around in her tired head until she was totally confused.

A few low-key complaints from the kitchen brought her thoughts back on track and she went to retrieve the twins, although dreading coming into contact with Nick. She let out a long breath in a relieved sigh when she found him absent from the kitchen and the twins almost asleep. She lifted them one at a time from their pram and put them to bed.

A quietness settled over the old house, broken only by an odd creak in the timbers. Grace lay back on the bed and eventually fell asleep. It was Sam who woke her at ten o'clock and as she changed him, hoisting him on to one hip while she got the bottles ready, she dredged up some common sense. Whatever reason Nick had for kissing her, at least he hadn't persisted when he'd realised that she was upset.

She thought of Karen: tall, curvaceous and bubbling with personality. There was no way Nick could be attracted to a skinny girl with bright red hair. The uneasy thought that he might have turned to her, simply because he'd been deprived of feminine company, was ruthlessly squashed. Forcing herself to be honest, she knew that Nick had no need to force himself on anyone. Frankly, he was far more likely to have women lining up to share his bed.

Sally joined in the chorus. 'I'll be back for you,' Grace called out.

'I'll take her.'

Grace jumped, giving Sam a thrill a minute. She gave Nick a curt nod. 'Thanks.'

They sat in silence, feeding the babies and then carrying them back to the nursery. Grace went through the bedtime ritual with the speed of light. She hoped the twins didn't feel short changed with the lightning kisses she bestowed on them, but being closeted in the small room with Nick had sent her nervous system into a tailspin.

Glad to escape an atmosphere charged with tension, she retreated to her bedroom, hoping that she would soon find relief from her problems in sleep.

Similarly affected, Nick decided to find solace in a good dose of caffeine, the evil-looking cup of coffee cooling on the kitchen table while he sat with his head propped in his hands. They'd only exchanged a kiss for God's sake. He'd lost count of the number of women he'd kissed, and in a far more sensual fashion than that. He hadn't often stopped at kissing either.

Damn, but she'd felt good in his arms! Not that she'd stayed there for long. He felt as if he'd had a taste of heaven, only to have it snatched away. Heaven. That was a joke. He wasn't called 'Old Nick' for nothing and his regular stamping ground sure wasn't paradise.

He straightened his shoulders and picked up the coffee. Keep away from her. He'd keep on repeating the words until they were engraved on his brain. Putting the cup to his lips he drank deeply. Ugh! In one movement he shoved his chair back and slung the coffee down the sink. As the syrupy black fluid gurgled down, he picked up the jar of instant coffee half expecting it to be labelled 'Poison'.

'Same thing,' he muttered as the word 'Decaffeinated' hit him. She must have brought it with her. He never touched the stuff. None of life's substitutes for him. It was all or nothing.

Immediately he pictured having it all with Grace. He

stifled a groan. His subconscious was having a field day and he had to take control. If her reaction was anything to go by, she wasn't into sexual relationships. Of course, maybe she just didn't fancy him…? His shoulders slumped at the thought as he took himself off to his bedroom.

The bed creaked alarmingly as he sat down and removed his shoes. He glanced around the room, changing the direction of his thoughts as he stood up and undressed. New furniture was a must – especially a new bed. Yep! Those are the sorts of things he should be concentrating on. Unfortunately, concentrating on a new bed didn't turn out to be such a good idea. Not when his mind was filled with thoughts of lying in a large, comfortable bed with Grace beside him.

'No!' The word boomed from his lips and he threw himself full length on the bed hoping that Grace hadn't heard. He took several deep breaths. In and out. That's it. Get a grip! As his nervous system simmered down, he paraded facts and figures through his mind.

He was thirty-five years old and, as far as the facts of life went, he had practically written the book. On the other hand, Grace's experiences probably wouldn't even fill one page! He went another round with his subconscious when it threw up a mental image of him enhancing Grace's knowledge.

Marshalling his wayward thoughts, he hammered them into shape. Grace and he had nothing in common. For one thing, just look at how she doted on those babies. While he still regarded them as something that could blow up in his face. Then there was that terrible experience with the dirty nappy. His stomach heaved at the memory. Grace changed them without batting an eyelid.

Nothing in common. He chanted the words like a mantra. Absolutely nothing in common. Besides, just look at the physical difference between. It would be like mating a Mack truck with a limousine. He let out a long breath. His nervous system was under control. Whew! Now he'd be able to get some sleep.

It couldn't be morning already. Nick groaned and looked at his watch. Six a.m. and his early morning call was in full cry. It was Sally. Now, how did he know that? He was no baby expert. His expertise was in other areas. Yeah! And last night it had been given full rein. He squirmed when he remembered the dreams he'd had. So much for mind over matter.

He lurched from a bed which resembled a war zone, the tumbled sheets and tousled pillows evidence of the rough night he'd put in. He paused in front of his bedroom mirror and reluctantly looked at the face that stared back at him, flinching at the red-eyed, stubble-jawed apparition which confronted him. Shuddering, he turned away from his reflection. Something had to be done.

Hard work – that was it. He'd put all his future plans into action and Miss Touch Me Not wouldn't know what had hit her. He quickly cast the remnants of last night's dreams aside. School boy stuff that, and if a little voice inside his head said how bloody good it was, he ruthlessly silenced it.

Grace watched as Nick spooned cereal into his mouth. He might as well have been on another planet. He'd avoided eye contact with her and she'd bet pounds to peanuts that he could just as easily have been eating sawdust.

Nick swallowed and Grace watched the firm muscles in his throat flex. She was trying to calm down her racing pulse and keep her toes from curling, when he finally broke the tense silence.

'Renovations.'

As a conversation starter it was well behind the eight ball. Grace nodded in encouragement.

He waved the spoon about. 'I'll put a boot behind the council today and get my plans through. This house is the pits.'

'It's a lovely old house,' Grace said.

'Rubbish! It's dark and gloomy and it needs a facelift. The rooms need opening up and the kitchen and bathrooms are archaic.'

Grace thought he was going to a lot of trouble for one person. He'd obviously planned the renovations before she'd come on the scene with the twins. A little glimmer of hope warmed her heart. Perhaps he'd decided to accelerate the process because he expected them to be around for a while?

'Someone needs to be on hand while the tradesmen work,' he said, his words slowly shattering her hopes. 'Might as well get things under way while you're here.'

He was gone in minutes, leaving a strange sense of emptiness behind. Her body seemed to go its own sweet way when he was around and she didn't need her life to be any more complicated than it was already. He certainly made his presence felt. She grinned. Someone should send the council a cyclone warning before he blasted their socks off.

Life settled into a pattern and Grace was surprised at how well she coped. Nick helped with feed time when he was home, and she devised ways of feeding them together when he wasn't. Shopping was a nightmare, but the supermarket agreed to deliver her phone order for a small charge.

Nick stuffed money into an old Toby jug on the shelf above the stove and, although it bothered her, Grace had no choice but to use it. He was working long hours and although he ate the dinner she kept hot for him, he bolted as soon as he'd finished the last mouthful. He retreated to the closed-in veranda which doubled as an office, only returning to help with the ten o'clock feed.

Sally lay like a little doll in his arms as he fed her and Grace wondered why he always fed the little girl and practically ignored Sam. She felt indignant on Sam's behalf, especially as he was the one who resembled Nick, in colouring at least. His thatch of black hair looked like a mini version of Nick's.

She wondered what Nick had looked like as a child. He was so essentially male and sometimes he looked as if he'd lived a thousand lifetimes.

'Do you have any photographs of yourself as a baby?' she asked.

Nick's head jerked up. 'No!'

There was a wealth of mystery behind that emphatic negative, but Grace decided it would be more than her life was worth to try to get to the bottom of it. He'd told her nothing of his background, but maybe it was better that way.

A heart to heart talk would lead to questions about her background and the events prior to the twins' arrival. And she wasn't ready to share that part of her life with Nick. Not with anyone.

'Surely you don't work on Sundays?' Grace took in Nick's appearance at the breakfast table. He wore a blue cotton shirt and grey slacks. The simple outfit shrieked designer work-wear and she couldn't believe he was going to work around the farm in expensive clothes.

'I'm an engineer, Grace, not a nine-to-five clerical worker. I've always worked long hours, until the project

I'm involved in is up and running.'

'You said that you had to mow the grass,' she said.

'And you sound like a nagging wife,' he threw back at her.

She did, she realised, and she really didn't care about the grass, even if it was ankle deep. The fact was, another day with just the twins for company would just about send her round the bend.

'Maybe I could do it,' she said.

The look he gave her would have curdled milk. 'I bought a ride-on mower suited to my proportions. It would literally make mincemeat of you, if you ended up under it.'

She shuddered. Machinery was something she had no affinity with. She stood up, gathering the breakfast dishes and stacking them noisily in the sink. 'Enjoy your day.'

Unfamiliar guilt flooded Nick's system. Great! Now he felt like slime, just because he was doing his job. He'd never had to consider others before and he shouldn't have to start now. No way! He hadn't asked her to land on his doorstep – and he wasn't prepared to rearrange his day for anyone.

'I'll probably be home at lunchtime.'

It was a toss up as to who was the most shocked at his words. Nick couldn't believe he'd said that. He'd intended to put in a full day's work at the factory and coming home at lunchtime had definitely not been on his agenda. For days he worked himself to a standstill, so that when he went to bed at night exhaustion took over. He'd relegated his erotic dreams to the back burner, but he had an uneasy feeling they were lurking in the wings, just waiting their chance to take centre stage.

He strode off to the makeshift garage. For the umpteenth time he cursed the day a red-haired dynamo, plus excess baggage, had landed on his doorstep. He didn't need the complications which she and the babies had brought with them. The sooner they left, the better he would be pleased.

Emotions surged through his system. Emotions which he had thought he'd battered to extinction: an urge to protect and nurture. A shaft of pain pierced his heart. His past efforts in that direction had ended in disaster. He thought of his brother Sam, before immediately banishing the thought to the far recess of his mind.

Pictures of the twins flashed through his brain and he could almost feel Sally's warm fuzzy head nestling against his neck. Memories of her brother's dark eyes reproached him. Why did he avoid contact with Sam? Was it because of the memories he triggered?

He put his hand on the car door and rested his head on the roof of the vehicle, stifling the groan that erupted from deep within his body. He felt as if he were teetering on the edge of a precipice and he was damned if he'd topple over. He'd been there, done that, and his strong character had carried him through.

Straightening his shoulders he flung open the door and threw himself behind the wheel. Nothing and no one would deter him from the goals which he had set for himself. He had a reputation for being a tough, ruthless bastard – so he might as well live up to it!

The factory was quiet and it was with a sense of satisfaction that he noted the progress he'd made. They would be starting production soon, and for him it was the fulfilment of a dream.

Entering his office he threw himself into his chair and stared moodily into space. He'd always thrived on challenge. Perhaps that's why he'd gone to foreign countries, undertaking the jobs that others wouldn't consider. He'd literally risked life and limb and, in doing so, he'd amassed a small fortune.

He couldn't pinpoint precisely when it had all gone wrong…when he'd realised that enough was enough. He put his head in his hands. Of course he could. It had been the accident that had killed Sam, which had put a shaft through his life. Then there was the bullet that had grazed his neck. That, too, had shaken him. He'd made a lot of plans for the future – dying wasn't one of them.

As soon as he thought of death, his thoughts turned again to Sam. His young brother's life had been cut short, and whenever he remembered the circumstances a little part of him died again. The familiar depression tried to take hold, but he was well versed by now in knowing how to combat it.

For the next few hours he worked at fever pitch, until he felt in total command of his thoughts. Work had always been his salvation and for those people who likened him to the devil, he could have told them that he continually did battle with a few of his own.

chapter five

As the Range Rover bumped along the rough driveway, Nick mentally added laying a bitumen track to his list of improvements. Grace was sitting under the jacaranda tree and he grinned as the sun shone on her bright hair. Firebrand. Fire! Heat! Damn this business of word association, because *he* was now hot. Oh, Lord – it was happening again! He pulled up in the barn and rested his head on the steering wheel.

Perhaps if he thought of something icy-cold, his renegade hormones would take a hike. He climbed out of the car and walked over to the tree, staying just out of range. He hoped her long-distance sight was lousy as he tried to cudgel his body into normality.

'I need a cold beer,' he called out. 'Do you want one?'

She leapt up. 'Let me get it. I'll just have cold water'

What else, he thought. 'No!' He hastened to keep her at a distance. 'I need a shower.' And ain't that the truth, he added grimly to himself. 'I'll bring the drinks out in a few minutes.'

He left her with the twins gurgling happily on the rug and flung himself into a cold shower. It took more than a few minutes to return to normal, but he was damned if he was going to allow any female to direct the hormonal beast that lay within.

Ice tinkled in the glass as he placed her cold water on a tray. He went to put his can of beer beside it, hesitating for a moment. It tasted damn good straight from the can, but he had a feeling that might offend Grace's sensibilities.

Sighing he picked up a crystal glass and put it beside the can. Henpecked? That'll be the day. The impulse, which had led him to the decision that he didn't want Grace to think of him as a slob, was ruthlessly denied. It was just a case of needing to set a good example to the twins. He picked up the tray and shook his head. He was definitely becoming a basket case.

As he trod down the front steps, he noted the grass. It would be blowing in the breeze soon. Mowing wasn't his favourite pastime, but soon he wasn't going to have a choice. He looked over at the tree. What in the hell was she doing?

Grace jumped up with a shriek and planted herself firmly in front of the twins. He followed the direction of her gaze and the tray went sailing through the air, the elegant crystal glass ending up shattered into small fragments.

Nick paused only to swiftly grab a stick as his long legs brought him close to the tree. The red-bellied black snake was coiled in an aggressive heap, only feet from Grace and the babies. In seconds its back was broken and Nick had flung the stick aside and scooped Grace into his arms.

'The twins,' she sobbed. 'Pick them up, please, Nick.'

Gently he thrust her aside and gathered a twin under each arm. They were still smiling. His heart hammered like a piston and he leaned back on the tree to get his breath.

'I hope it's not true that they come in pairs,' he gasped eyeing the mutilated shiny black mess in the grass.

Her eyes widened in alarm and he castigated himself for opening his big mouth. 'I'll cut the grass' he said. 'At least that should keep them away from the house.'

Grace sat at the kitchen table listening to the sound of the mower. He hadn't even had his beer or the sandwiches which she'd prepared earlier. She felt to blame. She should have had more sense. The twins were asleep, none the worse for the episode, but Grace felt inadequate both as a substitute mother and a person.

The only thing she could think of, when she'd seen the snake, had been to place herself between it and the babies. She remembered someone telling her to stay perfectly still, even if a snake slid over her foot. She didn't even know if she had that kind of courage and she shuddered to think of the outcome if Nick hadn't taken charge.

Her uneaten sandwich sat on the plate and eventually she stood up and threw it in the rubbish bin. The thought of being responsible for her sister's babies overwhelmed her at regular intervals. She just seemed to lurch from one crisis to another.

Through the window she could see Nick negotiating the big mower around trees, supremely confident in his ability. The ground was uneven and the mower bounced around. What if he came off? She remembered his words about making mincemeat of her. Her nervous system was still feeling ragged and suddenly she was afraid for him.

It seemed like hours before he finished mowing the large home paddock around the house, turning towards the barn to put the mower away. She watched him walking back to the house. His shorts were cut-off denim, exposing his strong tanned legs. He had an akubra, his favourite battered old hat, firmly clamped on his head. He was filthy and yet he absolutely screamed sex appeal.

Grace gulped. She couldn't…wouldn't…go down that path. It would be like trying to sail around the world without a compass. Men like Nick were as foreign to her as an alien life form.

It took an effort to quell her thoughts and racing heart, but she went to meet him at the back door, taking herself firmly in hand. Keep him at a distance, she told herself grimly. Her role was to offer some home comforts in return for the roof he provided over their heads. Nothing more.

His legs were a mass of small cuts and he had a bloody mark on his forehead. Her hand flew to her mouth and she rushed up to him, leaving about as much distance as would house a sheet of paper.

'You're hurt. Bleeding!' she cried out, clutching his arm as if she expected him to fall in a heap at her feet.

'Just the usual cuts and grazes inflicted by flying debris.'

'But, your head. It's bleeding quite badly.'

Moving from her grasp, he threw off his hat and wiped at his brow with a large hand. It came away quite bloodied and he looked surprised. 'That's from a stone. Gave me quite a wallop.'

'It needs attention. Where do you keep the first aid box?'

'It's nothing,' Nick protested. 'I need to shower again and change. By then it should have stopped bleeding.'

Grace opened her mouth to object, but his voice was terse and he sounded weary. 'I'm a big boy now, Grace. I can tend my own war wounds.'

He strode off leaving her emotions more messed up than ever. He was right, of course. He didn't need anyone to nursemaid him. He didn't need her or the twins and she was only deluding herself if she thought they had any role to play in his life.

There was probably nothing in his life that he couldn't cope with. He disposed of problems like fleabites. She shivered. He probably had some private investigator on the job, sorting out the twins' parentage or, even more likely, he was planning to take a DNA test. Once he could prove they weren't his, she and the twins would have to leave.

Nick let the hot water rush over his large frame. Yep! It looked as if he'd found the way to control his raging hormones. Every bone in his body ached and his head was beating like a tom-tom. He stood until the water ran cold. Just a precaution, of course, but the thought of Grace playing doctor nearly set him off again.

She was sitting at the kitchen table staring into space.

'Hello.' He knocked on the table. 'Anyone home?'

She smiled. 'You look squeaky clean.'

He gave her a long look. 'I'll never be that Grace.'

He knew she meant physically, but he didn't want her thinking – just because he couldn't bring himself to throw her out – that he was anything special. She might see him as her knight in shining armour, but she also had to see that his armour was dented and pitted from the scars of life.

'Your head? It's a nasty cut.'

'Nothing that a butterfly plaster won't put right.' He made a mental note to keep the first aid box in the bathroom where it belonged. He'd flung it in the kitchen cupboard when he first moved in.

As he found the box and took out the plaster she put out her hand. 'I'll do it.'

His internal battle was fierce, but too lengthy. She had the plaster out of his hand and on to his forehead, while he was still battering his body into submission.

'There, that should do it.'

Oh, Grace – if only you knew! The thought of 'doing it' was driving him crazy. He threw himself down on to the kitchen chair, welcoming the sudden weariness that flooded through him.

She put a plate of sandwiches and his cold beer in front of him. He looked at the can with suspicion. Would he? Should he?

'You don't want a glass do you?' she asked. 'Father always said it was better from the can.'

He laughed, remembering the fate of the crystal glass.

He'd always imagined Grace's parents to be very correct and dignified and he was glad to think her old man was a normal guy.

'Your Dad enjoyed a beer, did he?'

'I… he…' She swallowed quickly.

Now what could possibly be wrong with that question? Why should she suddenly be looking so depressed? Most fathers enjoyed a beer and she'd said that he drank it from a can.

'Yes. He did.'

The snake incident must have upset her. She reminded him of a young filly shying away from the bit. She was nervous all right. Hell! Maybe he hadn't hidden his more basic feelings as well as he thought?

'Thanks for lunch,' he said levering himself out of the chair. It was out to the office-cum-veranda again. At least there, he could be miserable in peace.

Grace spent what remained of the afternoon cooking special food for Sally and Sam. Just as she was trying to decide what to prepare for tea, Nick stuck his head around the door. 'Don't cook anything for me, Grace, I need to work through tonight. I can always make a snack if I get hungry.'

He disappeared back into his bolthole on the veranda and Grace let the suspicion that he was avoiding her take hold and grow. She sighed as she cleaned up the cooking utensils which she'd used to prepare the twins' food.

She couldn't deny the fact that she and the babies had disrupted his life in no small way, and at a time when he needed to concentrate on the developments in his life. He seemed to be in the throes of an enormous change in his lifestyle. He'd mentioned Saudi Arabia and she presumed he had spent most of his time as an engineer working away from Australia.

A puzzled frown knit her brow. To establish a factory in Queensland's Sunshine Coast hinterland indicated an intention to stay in one place. And then, there was the farmhouse. He would scarcely have bought and made plans to renovate it, if he hadn't intended to settle down.

No wonder he was edgy. A huge change in lifestyle was one thing, but to have the unexpected responsibility of fatherhood thrust upon him as well, would have given even the strongest nervous system a jolt. Grace gave the bench tops a savage wipe with the dishcloth as she wondered where it would all end.

Nick always arrived faithfully for the ten o'clock feed, settling down in the big leather chair with Sally cradled in his arms. Grace looked at the picture they made. The little girl lay back sucking hungrily at her bottle and Nick gave her the vestige of a smile.

Grace hid a grin. He didn't realise it, but there was a crack in the dam wall. However, he still displayed little interest in baby Sam, which irked the hell out of her. In fact, Sam was a gorgeous baby. But, it was almost as if Nick was scared of him…and that didn't make any sense. Perhaps she should challenge him and tell him that he fathered two children, not just one red-headed little girl?

No. Better to leave things as they were. Especially when she thought of all that he'd done so far. Patience was the name of the game. If everything worked out, then he would eventually come around to giving Sam equal attention. She puzzled over his attitude, but he was clearly a complex man striving to present a tough image to the world. Was he really so tough all the way through?

Nick took a cautious sip of his coffee. He glanced at a plunger on the table and let his breath out.

Grace watched the little episode and hid a smile. She knew all about his aversion to decaffeinated coffee. What he didn't need to know, was that it came in ground beans for the plunger. He hadn't detected the difference as he had with the instant coffee and Grace felt that she was making a small contribution to improving his health.

Confidently he took a large swig of the coffee. 'There'll be a couple of workmen coming today to start on the house.'

Grace set her own cup down on the table. Nothing like having plenty of warning! 'Today...?' she said, wondering what Chamber of Horrors lay ahead. 'Does this mean your plans have been approved?'

'More or less, but the work today doesn't involve regulations.' He took another deep draught of his coffee and the look on his face could only be described as self-satisfied. 'The wallpaper's coming off.'

'But, the twins...'

'I've organised that. The workmen will move their stuff into the lounge. It doesn't have wallpaper. The furniture in the other rooms can be covered in dust sheets. If necessary we can all camp in the lounge.'

Camping with Nick? It didn't matter where, just the thought was enough to make her blood fizz. She glanced at him. He looked perfectly normal. No excitement there. Her blood returned to normal. For him it was merely a practical solution. No happy families for him!

She smothered a sigh and raised the cup to her lips.

'I'll go,' he said as he rose to his feet, pushing his chair back and heading towards the door. He hesitated. 'That's nice coffee. Buy some extra and I'll take it to work.'

Grace choked and put her cup down. Nick came back and patted her on the back. 'Don't drink it so quickly.' He grinned. 'You're entitled to a meal break.'

He turned to leave once she'd recovered her breath, but she forestalled him. 'Wait! I've got an extra jar of the coffee in the pantry. You might as well take it with you.' As she collected the coffee she hid a grin, thankful that she had prudently put it in a jar and thrown away the packet 'decaffeinated' label.

He shoved the jar into his briefcase before leaving and she sat listening to the powerful throb of the car's engine as he drove down the track. The place seemed empty without him.

There was no question of empty now, Grace thought, as Dan and Joe threw furniture around and covered what still remained in place.

Dan was the mover and shaker and Joe followed orders. 'He's my young brother,' Dan explained. There are six of us. Joe and I work in Dad's renovating business. He's got two more sons to come.'

'Any daughters?' Grace pitied the outnumbered females in the household, but Dan's rapt expression soon made her revise her opinion.

'The twins,' he said. 'Only five and gorgeous.'

Grace had put Sally and Sam safely out of the way in Nick's makeshift office, but Dan was quick on the uptake.

'Two cots,' he said. 'Two babies.' His face took on a dreamy look. 'Twins?'

'Yes.' Grace wished Nick would look like that. Some hope.

'Where?'

'Out on the veranda,' Grace said.

Dan was on his way before she could give directions. He had Sam up in his arms and Grace wished that she had a camera.

Perhaps being one of six ensured that Dan had an affinity

with children, but he seemed like a natural to her. He studied Sam's face and nodded. 'Looks like the boss,' he announced.

'You've actually met Nick?' Grace asked.

'Just the once, but I never forget a face. Your husband leaves quite an impression.' A grin split his homely face. 'Big bloke, isn't he. This fellow will be just like him. Look at his big feet.'

'He has got big feet hasn't he?' She'd never really noticed before. Her confidence and hopes soared. Sam had Nick's dark hair, and he was a big baby. He had the potential to grow into a gorgeous, sexy hunk, just like his father. She turned away quickly. She could feel her face positively glowing. What was wrong with her? Since moving in with Nick, her thoughts were continually shocking her.

It was as if she had embarked on a new journey. She had certainly come to a stumbling halt on the old one, despite years of anticipation and preparation. Suddenly she felt apprehension. If on this journey she was following in Nick's footsteps, she could just end up in Purgatory.

Dan was putting Sam back in the pram.

'I'll make you and Joe a cup of tea,' she said.

They were sitting around the table laughing and drinking tea when Nick strode in.

With a look that would have guaranteed incineration he asked about the morning's progress.

'Well, boss,' said Dan without turning a hair. 'I reckon we're ahead of schedule.'

'That right?' Nick's comment left nothing to the imagination and Grace held her breath.

Dan and Joe got the message, thanked her for the tea and went back to work.

'They're here to work, not drink bloody tea,' Nick said.

'Oh, really…?' Grace said. 'Do your staff at the factory

work non-stop? And exactly where do you keep your whip?'

'My *what*…?' He leaned close to her. 'Listen, Miss Smarty Pants – my staff have regular breaks, but they don't waste time fooling around.'

'Neither do Joe and Dan. They've worked non-stop.' Grace drew in a sharp breath. Nursing Sam could hardly be called fooling around. Or could it? Just what did he mean by that, anyway?

'What are you doing here?' she asked.

'I live here.'

'Yes, but you *never*…' she placed heavy emphasis on the 'never', '…come home during the day.'

'Perhaps I should,' he said.

'What's that supposed to mean?' Her mind was right into imagination mode. Surely he didn't think…?

'You and I know zilch about each other, Grace. You could be up to anything while I'm away.'

'That's a beastly thing to say. In case you hadn't noticed, I've got two very effective chaperones.'

'Yes,' he agreed. 'I would have to admit that they might be a little off-putting.'

Off-putting! So that's what he thought of those two beautiful children. She'd give him *off-putting*!

She stood up, stepping towards him. 'Now that you've discovered that the heinous crime of drinking tea has been committed in your house, you can go and terrorise your other employees,' she said.

Nick wasn't sure if he felt amused or outraged. He was about to be thrown out of his own house by a miniature bouncer.

'Since when did you start flinging orders around?' he growled.

'Since… since…' She obviously wasn't prepared to

back down. 'Blame it on the school teacher in me.'

'School teacher!' She looked more like a pupil than a teacher. He could teach her a thing or two. On no! Not those fantasies again. 'You didn't tell me you were a teacher.'

'You didn't ask.'

'What else should I be asking, Grace?'

'Nothing. I haven't any dark past and what I am doesn't affect my usefulness to you. I look after your babies, do the domestic chores and now it looks as if I've been appointed to keep your galley slaves under control!'

That last shot was a hit below the belt and he bit back at her. 'You seem to have forgotten something. We have yet to establish that I am the father of the twins.'

'Even Dan thinks Sam looks like you.'

She hadn't meant to say that, he could see by the dismay on her face.

She had some gall. 'Do you have to parade my alleged misdemeanours for everyone to pass judgement on?'

She looked genuinely shocked. 'Those babies are not misdemeanours. Besides Dan thinks that you're my husband.'

'You wish!' he said.

It was definitely the wrong thing to say. Especially to a fiery redhead. She was immediately squaring up to him, her cheeks blazing.

'You got that wrong, Nick Best. Marriage to you would be a fate worse than death – and I don't have a death wish!' She turned and marched out, leaving him feeling as if he'd gone ten rounds with Muhammad Ali.

He didn't have a death wish either. Marriage. Hell! It had nothing going for it. Imagine living a lifetime with Grace. Imagine it...his mind threw back at him, accompanied by a list of fringe benefits that frightened him silly.

chapter six

Grace watched as he hurled himself into the Rover and drove off. It's a wonder the car didn't become airborne as he shot down the drive ignoring the potholes he usually carefully avoided.

She hadn't thought Nick Best would be afraid of anything, but the word marriage had him running scared. He didn't need to worry about her. Marriage had never figured in her plans. Well, not exactly.

Everything was such a mess. If Nick kept the babies it would be better if he did marry. Children needed a mother. The thought of anyone else mothering the twins was not to be tolerated. So where did she go from here?

Pictures flashed through her mind like the scenes in a movie. Nick and her as a couple sharing the twins' upbringing. The lovely old farmhouse renovated with her as its mistress. New bedroom furniture of course. She bit her lip. Stop right there. Whatever she envisioned in the bedroom was never going to happen. She tried to put a stop to her rampaging thoughts, but they went around and around in her head until she developed a headache.

One step at a time. She'd learned to do that the hard way. At the moment she and the twins had a roof over their heads and she could repay Nick by running the house and supervising the renovations.

In a couple of days the wallpaper was off and the rooms were ready for painting. Nick's suggestion that they camp in the lounge became a reality as the smell of paint drove them from the bedrooms.

He produced a couple of blow-up beds and put them on the lounge floor. 'Sorry about the lack of privacy. I could go out on the veranda, but the mosquitoes would carry me off.'

'There's no need for that,' Grace said. If it hadn't been for the twins and the fact that she often had to get up to them she would have braved the mosquitoes herself.

It wasn't that she didn't trust Nick, especially as he'd made it clear that she held no attraction for him. The attraction he held for her was her major problem. For the first time in her life her body seemed to be ruling her head and she hated the experience.

She reasoned with herself. Hadn't she always tried to take a mature, logical approach to coping with adversity? Oh sure! What about her decision to leave the babies on Nick's doorstep? Very mature, that.

While she acknowledged that her poor physical state had definitely influenced her thinking at that time she didn't have that as an excuse at the moment. Despite the uncertainty of the future just having Nick to share the responsibility even on a temporary basis had definitely given her some breathing space.

As she slid into her makeshift bed clad in one of her plain white nighties she set her mind to overcoming her problem. Perhaps her physical state did have a bearing on the situation, but it had nothing to do with a lack of food and everything to do with overactive hormones and it certainly wasn't going to be allayed by sharing anything with Nick.

She tried to brainwash herself. There was nothing attractive about Nick. His very size was a turn off. She remembered the strength of his strong arms when he'd held her. How he'd dealt with the snake. OK. There were instances when his size was an asset, but as a lover his bulk would be frightening.

He would never be her lover. She drummed the words into her head. She changed tack. He wasn't all that good looking unless dark craggy men turned you on. Of course his near black eyes were rather compelling. She thought of the way they danced on the few occasions when he'd been amused about something. When he was angry she felt sure she would fall into their depths never to be seen again.

She dismissed his eyes. There was his thick black hair with its ridiculous streak of silver. It made him stand out in a crowd. Distinctive, her recalcitrant mind suggested.

Grace knew when to give up. She shoved the pillow over her face. It was mind over matter and she could do that. The next time she saw Nick he would have no affect on her at all. She lifted the pillow off her face and her heart nearly stopped in its tracks.

'You'll have to put up with the old shorts,' he said, as he came into the room clad in what had once been a pair of football shorts. 'I don't own any pyjamas.'

She nodded. Every ounce of breath was needed to keep her lungs inflated. His legs were gorgeous. Long and well shaped. Her eyes travelled up to his broad chest smattered with black curly hair. His naturally olive skin still bore the tan he'd acquired from years spent outdoors. Even to her untutored palate he was sex appeal on two legs.

Oblivious to the state of her nervous system he wished her a good night. 'Hope you don't mind roughing it. I'm used to it. Could sleep on a bed of nails.'

That statement was shot to pieces when Grace heard him thundering about the kitchen in the early hours of the morning. She dragged herself out of bed. The twins were sound asleep and she hadn't expected to play nursemaid to Nick. Perhaps he was hungry and needed a snack.

He was sitting at the kitchen table with his head in his hands. There was no evidence of a snack and if his dejected pose was anything to go by food was the last thing on his mind.

Grace's stomach lurched. He couldn't be sick. He seemed indestructible. With frightening accuracy she remembered a newspaper article which had outlined the death of men in their thirties from heart attack. She panicked. He ate the most terrible food when he got the chance.

'Nick!'

He looked up wincing with pain. She raced over dropping on to the chair beside him. 'Where does it hurt? Tell me.'

'My head. I've got the father of all headaches – and there's no bloody paracetamol.'

It was the last thing she expected him to say. Her mind went into overdrive again. Cerebral Haemorrhage. 'How long?' she asked. 'How long has your head been aching?'

He looked at her blankly. 'I don't know. Off and on for a day or two, but it was bearable until tonight.'

'Can you think of anything that caused it? Did you bump your head?'

'No! I didn't bump my head. I haven't got a hangover. I've drunk nothing stronger than coffee for ages.'

Coffee! Oh God! Grace thought guiltily of the jar of decaffeinated coffee that he had gone off to work with days ago. He didn't know it, but he'd had no caffeine for days and he must have been suffering from withdrawal symptoms.

'I've got some paracetamol,' she said. As she rummaged through her handbag she toyed with the idea of making him a cup of 'real coffee', but decided that as he'd inadvertently gone through 'cold turkey', she'd better leave well alone.

He was so grateful, and she felt terrible.

'God, I'm late.' Nick leapt up out of his makeshift bed on the floor and Grace waited, holding her breath, to see if he had recovered from his headache.

'Better?' she asked.

He looked puzzled. 'Oh, the headache. Yes, its gone, thank goodness.' He went off to the bathroom mumbling about earthquakes and bullet wounds, none of which resulted in a headache.

Bullet wounds? Grace felt her blood run cold. Had he actually been shot at? Her spirits sank to an all time low. They obviously had nothing in common. In fact, the disparity between their lifestyles was enormous. The thought that he was probably quite capable of returning the gunfire depressed her even further. Especially when she had difficulty squashing even a bug.

She settled the twins in the baby bouncers Nick had bought. He was good at problem solving she had to admit. She sat between them on the floor and gave them their bottles. Sam invariably finished first, so she burped him and propped Sally's bottle to forestall the bellow of rage that inevitably followed an interrupted feed.

'They'll be getting down to the nitty-gritty today.' Nick had appeared towelling his hair dry. He wore the disreputable towelling robe that left nothing to the imagination.

'I mean with the renovations,' he added when she looked puzzled. He slung the towel on a chair and picked Sally up to burp her. She nestled into the side of his neck her head looking over his shoulder.

'Is she asleep?' Nick asked. 'She feels very relaxed.'

While Grace's mind grappled with the thought that nestling into Nick's neck would be the last way to relax, he turned around so that she could answer his question. She stood on tiptoe to get a better look at Sally. The scar on Nick's neck was quite visible. It looked like something had torn a piece of the flesh away. Grace sucked in her breath. A bullet? He *had* been shot!

'Hullo!' Nick swung back around. 'I think you're the one who went to sleep.'

'Sorry. I couldn't see her eyes properly. She isn't asleep.'

'Damn. I thought I had the magic touch.'

'She's only just woken up,' Grace pointed out. She put both the twins back in the bouncers and went to get breakfast.

Nitty-gritty was right, Grace thought, as she tried to shut out the noise of power saws and hammer drills. They were ripping out the odd wall and enlarging window openings.

'Of course the kitchen and bathroom are both to go. They'll be completely remodelled,' Dan said.

'Of course,' Grace said faintly.

'Have you and your husband chosen the fittings yet?'

'Er…no. Not yet.' Now was as good a time as any to tell Dan the truth, but it was complicated and would take some time. Remembering Nick's aversion to her distracting the workmen she said nothing.

Every morning Dan gave her a preview of the work to be done that day which was more than Nick did. At least it gave her a chance to work around the commotion that tearing the house apart caused.

It was the dust that was the biggest problem and Grace had to continually shift the twins to keep them in a comfortable environment. Her days were filled with stress and she didn't feel she could off-load her problems on Nick when he came home. She had chosen to invade his space and he would probably be very quick to remind her of that fact.

Nick seemed more interested in the progress being made

at the factory than on the home front. He probably thinks the washing and the ironing does itself, Grace thought angrily, as she snatched the clean washing from the line before Dan started up another machine to create a dust storm.

The basket was piled high and as Grace struggled along the veranda she realised that she was 'flying blind'. Not that she wasn't familiar with the landscape. The twins generated an enormous amount of washing and she made the journey to the clothesline more than once a day.

With her mind fully occupied with what she'd like to do to Nick if she had the courage, Grace failed to notice that Dan had added a couple of extension leads to her territory since her excursions the previous day.

Dan's head snapped up at her startled cry and he was just in time to witness a swallow dive over the clothes basket that would have earned her a place in the Olympic team. Unfortunately she'd done what all good divers do and landed headfirst.

Dan dropped his tools and scooped her up. 'Talk to me,' he muttered. 'Just say something. Anything.'

Nick sat back in his office chair and viewed the factory floor through the strategically placed window. He positively vibrated with satisfaction as he watched his staff moving efficiently about their business. They worked as a team and not only were they turning out quality products, but so far they all seemed to find satisfaction in their work. He'd done it. One of his dreams had come to fruition without too many hitches. Life was pretty good.

His thoughts swung to home, the twins and Grace. There were a few problems there. Now that the factory was up and running he could no longer use that as an excuse to shunt all his other problems in the 'too hard' basket. Was

Sam the twins' father and if he was how would he deal with that? He couldn't turn his back on his brother's children. He sighed. Fatherhood wasn't something he'd planned on. He had reservations about parenthood. Strong reservations.

Of course the whole issue could probably be resolved by some kind of test. DNA maybe? Although with Sam dead that could be difficult. So why was he putting it off? His mind skittered away from the issue. Perhaps he didn't really want to know and if that were the case why? A whole host of scenarios flooded his mind. If the babies weren't Sam's could he throw Grace and the twins out? Despite his hardboiled reputation he knew that would take some doing – and if they were Sam's would they carry on with the same arrangement? He shoved his thoughts and problems to the back of his mind and concentrated on his achievements on a professional level.

He glanced again at the factory floor, his spirits lifting at the thrum of activity. There were no issues here that he couldn't handle and as far as he could see that would be the case at home. Whatever happened he would find a way to cope.

The phone rang and he stretched lazily to pick it up.

'The missus has knocked herself out. You'll have to come home.'

Wrong number, Nick thought. No. That distinctive drawl was Dan's trademark.

'She's not…' Not a good time to clear up his marriage status, Nick decided.

'She's not making any sense,' Dan said.

'Is she unconscious?' Nick said. His stomach did a few unfamiliar somersaults as the seriousness of Dan's words sunk in. No need to panic. People knocked themselves out all the time. Yeah! They fractured skulls and suffered brain damage.

'Not now. Are you coming home or do I ring the ambulance?'

Nick caught the note of censure. 'I'm on my way.'

Something about Dan got right under his skin. Of course he was intending to go home. And she's not my missus, he chanted, as he broke the speed limit to reach the farm in record time. His hands clenched on the steering wheel. There was nothing to her. What if she had fractured her skull?

Pulling the big car to a screaming halt, Nick threw himself up the veranda steps and into the lounge. The picture of Dan sitting on the floor feeding the twins brought him to a sudden standstill. Nick threw a frantic glance around the room, sagging with relief when he saw Grace lying on the big leather sofa. That relief quickly turned to dismay when he noted her pale colour. Bending over her he gently brushed back a swatch of thick red hair, biting off an angry oath as he noted the redness and ugly swelling already evident from the blow she had sustained.

'I'm OK,' she said. 'Just a bit dizzy.'

'Gave herself a hell of a bang,' Dan offered from his position on the Persian rug. 'You'll need to take her to the hospital.'

I know that, Mr Know It All! Nick bit back the words. No sense in alienating the only person who could mind the twins. 'Right,' he said, determined to take charge of his own household. 'Let's go Gracie.'

Grace's eyes widened at the 'Gracie'. That was a first. 'I don't need the doctor. Just a few minutes rest.'

'You need a doctor,' both Nick and Dan said in unison.

She lay back and closed her eyes. Nick noticed the slight trembling of her limbs and had a sudden urge to hold her close. No way. He knew what being close to her did to him. One casualty was enough.

'She can't walk in that state,' Dan pointed out.

Nick resisted the urge to shake Dan until his teeth rattled down his throat, before sliding his arms under Grace. So much for keeping his hands off her. As her head flopped on to his shoulder, concern for her well-being drove any carnal thoughts from his mind. She really was hurt and guilt flooded his system. Particularly at having blithely organised the renovations, without giving any real thought to the extra burden it had placed on Grace.

As he went to leave the room Dan looked him in the eye, 'I can take care of the babies unless you want me to take Grace to the hospital.'

Nick felt his blood pressure surge as he realised he had taken Dan's help for granted, and he was being subtly reminded of the fact. There was a reprimand in there somewhere, as well. That Dan thought he was remiss in his duties as a father and husband was obvious. Telling him the truth would only thrust him deeper into the mire so, for almost the first time in his life, Nick kept his aggression to himself.

'If you could mind the twins, it would be appreciated.' Nick ground the words out, hoping that he sounded civil when his thoughts were homicidal.

'Mild concussion. Bed rest for a day and then ease back into your normal way of life.' The doctor looked at Nick reassuringly. 'Your wife will be back to normal in no time.'

Nick opened his mouth and shut it again. His wife. Every last citizen was determined to lumber him with a wife. What the hell. He and Grace knew the score.

'Come on, sweetheart,' he said, deciding to play the part.

'There's no need to go overboard,' Grace said as they got into the car.

'True,' said Nick. 'We both know where we stand.'

'Sure,' Grace said. 'You're the boss and I'm one of the galley slaves!'

'I resent that,' Nick said. 'I don't expect you to work yourself into the ground.'

'That's good to hear,' Grace said, leaning back in her seat. Her head was pounding and she felt slightly ill. 'Especially as I'm going to be out of action for twenty-four hours.'

A long silence greeted that statement and Grace closed her eyes. Her mind was seething with problems, but she simply didn't have the energy to sort them out.

Nick had the energy, but the solutions evaded him. For a moment he felt swamped, before clamping firmly down on his feelings of panic. Twenty-four hours was a lifetime – if it had to be spent minding two babies whose mouths resembled baby birds, and who left unspeakable deposits in their nappies.

He reached home and packed Grace off to bed. 'I can cope,' he said, not believing a word. Dan! Suddenly Dan seemed like the answer to a prayer.

Dan was winding up the extension leads when Nick tracked him down.

'Twins are asleep,' he volunteered.

Nick's smile would have done a crocodile proud. 'Thanks,' he said. 'I really appreciate your help.'

'Pity you don't appreciate your wife.'

Nick clenched his fists. *She's not my damn wife* he wanted to shout from the rooftop, but he knew when he was on the back foot.

'I *do* appreciate her,' he said with clenched teeth. 'That's why I want her to rest tomorrow. Grace trusts you with the babies. How about if you forget the renovations tomorrow, and take care of the twins?'

Dan looked at Nick for a long moment. 'Sorry,' he said.

'No can do. We're pouring a foundation on another site tomorrow and it's all hands on deck. Dad would nail my hide to a wall if I wasn't available.'

Nick's equilibrium went severely off balance. 'Whose going to mind the twins?' he blurted out.

Dan's smile was in a class of its own. 'You need the practice, boss? You do it.'

chapter seven

Nick was up off his mattress and on his feet before reality struck. Something had woken him. He glanced at his watch. Five-thirty in the morning. The chorus started up again and he looked, bleary eyed, to where the twins lay protesting loudly at the empty state of their stomachs.

Grace sat up on the leather sofa where she'd fallen asleep the night before. Nick looked hopefully in her direction, but as she groaned and put her head in her hands he knew that he was out of luck.

'I'll feed them,' he announced with false confidence. He strode into the kitchen and plucked two bottles out of the sterilising solution.

'Teats,' he muttered, 'got to have those.' He fished around and found them and the plastic rims which held them in place.

His meagre knowledge fizzled out at that point. 'Grace…what goes in the bottle?'

'Formula.'

He peered into the depths of the fridge.

'It's in a tin on the shelf above the fridge.'

The picture of a smiling baby helped with instant location. False advertising, he thought – just listen to that pair out there! He was about to roar out for more instructions, when he noted that the tin held a mine of information.

Triumphantly he strode into the lounge clutching the two filled bottles. He was about to hoist Sally, who despite being the smallest made the most noise, from her cot when Grace spoke.

'You've made them the right temperature, of course?'

Of course, nothing. 'Room temperature?' he said. 'I used tap water.'

'No!'

He almost dropped his precious bottles.

'Nick, you have to use boiled water from the kettle, and then you have to warm the bottles in hot water. The instructions were on the can.'

He raced back to the kitchen, with her warning to get two fresh bottles ringing in his ears. Yeah! The instructions *were* on the can, but he had foolishly decided the town water supply would be pure enough without further treatment. *Sheez*! Who would have thought that feeding two babies would be so complicated?

He repeated the process, following Grace's instructions and hoping that he wouldn't suffer premature deafness from the noisy environment. He shook his head. He could work and remain calm in an office situated in a factory that thrived on noise. Machinery, the sound of trucks revving their engines, the hubbub of human activity all did nothing to a nervous system, which seemed to descend into total disarray when a small baby cried.

Feeding two babies at once defied all knowledge gained from two university degrees, and if Grace hadn't volunteered to feed Sam, Nick felt that a total breakdown was only a hairsbreadth away.

The twins lay happily with Grace on the sofa while Nick got breakfast. He brought a tray into the lounge with two bowls of cereal, coffee and toast.

'You'll be late for work,' Grace said as she ate her cereal.

'I'm not going.'

'Not going?' She dropped her spoon back in the bowl.

She didn't have to sound as if the world was coming to an end!

'It's only one day, Grace. If I can establish communications networks in the wilds of the world in searing heat, I can mind two babies for a day.'

'Of course,' Grace said. She gave him a smile that would have rocked his socks if he'd been wearing any.

He picked up his spoon and began to eat his cereal.

'I've changed them,' she said. 'While you were getting breakfast.'

He choked on his cereal. Changing them had never occurred to him. Perhaps that would be it for the day. Information about the elimination of waste products seemed vital. 'Er… how many times a day do they need changing?'

'At least after every feed,' Grace said, adding hastily as he looked like running for cover, 'I can manage to do that.' His relief was almost comical as he pushed his cereal bowl to the side and bit into a piece of toast. 'I'll leave bathing them to you though. I might get dizzy and they need to be held firmly.'

The toast turned to ash in his mouth. He'd rather walk over hot coals than bath a baby. He pumped himself up. Where's your intestinal fortitude, Best? He thought of the men he'd had under his management. A rag-tag bunch of misfits at times. He'd whipped them into a force to be reckoned with *and* brought difficult assignments in on time.

Bathing two babies would be a breeze.

He hadn't expected it to involve so much preparation. The table was covered in a mountain of towels, clean clothes, baby wipes – and, of course, the baby bath.

'Stick your elbow in the water to test the temperature,' Grace told him. 'It might be old-fashioned, but it works.'

'My hide's as thick as an elephant. It could still be too hot,' he pointed out.

Grace sighed, rummaging in the drawer for a

thermometer. She placed it on the table along with a bottle of olive oil.

Nick gave the bottle an exasperated glance. 'I'm going to bath them not cook them,' he said.

'It helps to stop their skin drying out,' Grace said.

She sank back on the kitchen chair as she spoke and Nick felt guilty. The bang on the head had knocked her around. And so had working herself to a standstill, in a house that at the moment resembled the local tip, he admitted reluctantly.

He put his guilt on the back burner. He was doing his best under difficult circumstances. His self-esteem went up a few notches. Hell! He'd taken time out from running a new venture to look after two babies. This fatherhood role was all new to him. When the thought crossed his mind that he was putting himself through hoops for someone else's babies, he positively glowered.

His scowl was not lost on Grace. In a way, she couldn't blame him. Operating in a totally foreign environment did nothing for one's confidence. Instinctively, she knew that it would have been a lifetime ago when Nick Best had last felt the faintest stirrings of insecurity.

'Pour some of the olive oil into the bath water,' she instructed. 'Now pick up whichever twin you intend bathing first. They both love their bath, so there's no problem.'

Of course, he would pick up Sally first, but he was used to handling her so it was probably a good decision.

'Now undress her and roll her in a towel.'

'That doesn't make sense,' Nick said. 'She won't even be wet.'

'No, but you need to wash her head and you don't want her throwing herself around.'

'Head!' Nick looked at Sally's head as if it were a time

bomb. 'It's all soft and squashy,' he said. 'I can't wash it.'

'Of course you can.' Grace fought down the feelings of exasperation. She longed to go back and lie down, but Nick hadn't even started yet and his panic was only marginally contained.

She could almost see the internal battle as he undressed Sally, grasped her firmly and wrapped her in a towel.

'Hold her over the tub,' she said. 'Relax, Nick, it's not the Grand Canyon. It's only a bathtub!'

Gingerly he soaped and rinsed the bright red hair and then, with a heavy sigh of relief, he placed Sally back on the table.

'Now remove the towel and put your arm under her shoulder, holding the top of her arm. Put the other hand underneath her and grasp her leg, then lower her into the water.'

His confidence riding high, Nick did as he was asked – even managing to soap the little girl and rinse her off. He lifted her out and she almost shot out of his grasp. With a horrified yelp, he clasped her tightly to his chest.

As he expelled his breath, he looked at Grace with a twisted smile. 'Slippery little suckers, aren't they?'

'It's the oil. I should have warned you.'

'Yes, you damned well should have! I might have dropped her.'

By the time Sally was dressed and handed over to Grace, Nick was on a roll. Sam was soaped, rinsed and dressed in half the time, and Nick found himself literally left 'holding the baby'.

As he sat down with the little boy in his arms, Sam smiled a gummy smile and Grace watched as Nick swallowed uncomfortably. His arms tightened imperceptibly and she felt that maybe Sam had at last dented Nick's iron-clad resistance.

Memories flooded back before Nick could staunch the flow. He had adored his younger brother Sam – and he had killed him. Oh, it hadn't been deliberate. Never that. Even now, with the benefit of hindsight, the guilt all but consumed him.

He'd always looked out for Sam, despite the fact that his brother was reckless, spoiled and the child on whom his mother and father had doted. Nick bit back a sigh. He should have been jealous, and in fact he had been. But, Sam had been a lot younger and Nick, mature for his years, found that looking after Sam had become second nature.

He'd always felt a distance between himself and his parents; particularly his father. It didn't take a mathematician to work out that his mother had been pregnant with him before they were married, and he'd always imagined that his father had resented marriage being forced upon him.

Nick had never been able to overcome a deep-seated feeling of rejection and, if it hadn't been for his Uncle Will, he would probably have become another rebellious teenage statistic.

Grace watched the emotions playing over Nick's face and she felt afraid. He was hurting, deep down, and it was in some way connected with the baby, Sam. She put Sally down on a rug on the floor and reached for Sam, relieved when Nick silently handed him over. The legs of the chair scraped on the floor as he stood up, quickly striding from the room.

The day was hot and humid, but he seemed oblivious of that fact as he strode away from the house. Grace drew in a sharp breath as she watched him reach the fence line. He leaned his elbows on a post and looked away into the distance. It seemed to Grace that he was looking back in time, and that what he was seeing was making him deeply unhappy.

Sam was snuggling into her shoulder and Grace tore her glance away from Nick. How would she know what he was thinking? Perhaps he was just admiring the scenery. She shuddered remembering the look of pain as he'd held Sam.

Sam looked at her and beamed. Grace held her breath for a moment. How could such a beautiful child instil fear into another human being? His own father! Perhaps that was it? It *was* just possible that Nick wanted a son, but until he was sure that Sam was his own child, he would be afraid to love him.

Surely that same reasoning would apply to Sally, although often men had an entirely different emotional response to their daughters. Thoughts and explanations churned around in Grace's head making her headache ten times worse. It was all guesswork and Nick's reaction was clearly more than just reticence at becoming attached to his son.

She watched as he levered himself off the fence and walked away in the distance. A shiver passed over her as the thought that he was walking out of her life took hold.

Chastising herself for being too imaginative Grace turned away from the window. His property consisted of several acres so he had plenty of room to walk off his depression, if that's what it was. The original farm had been broken up and sold as five-acre blocks when the owner died, and his widow had gained permission to subdivide her land.

Grace realised how little she knew about Nick. Why had he chosen to live on an old farm? Why had he given up working overseas? And, if he had family, why did he never mention them? One day she might get up enough courage to ask.

But, even as the thought entered her mind, she gave a quick shake of her head. No. No, she wouldn't be doing that – not unless she was prepared to reveal the details of her own background, and she couldn't see that happening. Bringing up the twins had forced her problems to the back of her mind, but the confusion and loss of self-esteem was still there.

Nick was gone for a couple of hours. Grace spent the time amusing the twins and preparing some lunch. Realising that her improved health might be temporary, she decided to cook a casserole which they could eat for tea. It was cooking slowly in the old oven, filling the kitchen with the smell of mushroom and herbs when Nick appeared.

'Smells good,' he said going to the sink and filling a glass from the tap that supplied them with rainwater from the tank.

'I've made a beef and mushroom casserole for tea,' Grace said retrieving a tray of sandwiches which she had prepared for lunch. She placed them in front of him and put the kettle on to make his coffee.

He didn't offer any explanation for suddenly disappearing for a while and, as he sat at the table and took one of the sandwiches, he glanced around the room. 'Where are the babies?'

Grace waved her arm in the direction of the lounge. 'They went to sleep.'

The kettle whistled shrilly and when she moved towards the stove to make the coffee the room began to spin.

Nick dropped the sandwich and caught her as she began to sway. Scooping her up into his arms, he carried her into the lounge and put her gently on the sofa.

'Grace!' She looked like death and he gave full rein to several years' accumulation of pithy oaths. It acted like an electrical prod and her eyes flew open.

'Thank God!' he breathed.

'I'm surprised to hear you say that,' she muttered. 'Especially as, just a few seconds ago, you were taking his name in vain.'

'I thought that you'd passed out.'

Grace ran a hand wearily through her curls. 'No, I just had a dizzy spell.'

Nick leaned over her, placing a large calloused hand on her brow. 'I think I should take you back to the doctor.'

'No! I'm perfectly all right,' Grace insisted. 'I just feel a bit fragile, that's all.'

Nick stroked her hair away from her face. 'You're not wrong – fragile is the perfect description. But you always look as if a puff of wind would carry you off.'

The sofa dipped alarmingly as he sat down beside her, taking one of her slender hands in his.

'I'm sorry, Grace,' he hesitated. 'I'm sorry about taking off like that. I should never have left you to cope on your own. I just needed a bit of breathing space.'

She drew in a deep breath. 'It's something to do with Sam, isn't it?' she murmured, feeling as if she were walking through a minefield. But surely it was better to get the problem out into the open?

For several seconds it appeared that he wasn't going to answer. When he disengaged his hand from hers, she felt the distance which he was creating beginning to yawn between them. It was more emotional than physical, and when he spoke it was in a flat tone devoid of any feeling.

'Yes. It is to do with Sam. But not our little twin.'

Grace bit down on her bottom lip to stop any sound from emerging. The 'our' had touched her heart. He had said it unconsciously and for the first time she began to hope that he regarded Sam as his own child.

'I don't understand,' she began…

'I had a brother, Sam,' he said. 'He was killed in Saudi Arabia several months ago.'

'Oh, Nick, I'm so sorry.' Grace reached out and took his hand in both of hers and brought it to rest against her cheek.

Nick felt the acceleration of his heartbeat as his fingers touched her soft satiny skin. She lay back on the pillows with his hand cradled against her cheek and he could feel the comfort she was offering slowly flowing through his body.

Nick closed his eyes, moving his fingers gently over Grace's cheek. It was like tapping into her quiet strength; her sweetness and her compassion. She moved his hand slightly and pressed her lips into his palm. His eyes flew open and his feelings shifted up a gear. His distress was fading to be replaced with a more powerful emotion – and one that he had no more control over than his earlier melancholy.

Moving his hand, he slid his arm under her shoulders, lifting her towards him. Her arms wound around his neck and he kissed her gently on the mouth. Her response was unexpectedly sweet, but it carried the kick of a mule. Nick felt his body respond savagely and, for the first time in his life, he felt uncertain, almost afraid of the direction he was taking.

In seconds, his memory had provided him with a rapid replay of all the women he'd made love to. He'd never felt any uncertainty with them. And now he was aware of an unfamiliar sense of shame as he realised he'd had no hesitation in taking what they'd offered, despite the fact that he'd never felt more than a passing fancy for any of them.

He eased back slightly looking into Grace's eyes. They were shut tightly, but as he broke the kiss they opened wide, and he found himself gazing down into unfathomable, deep green pools. Gently he kissed her eyes shut, letting his mouth wander over her face, the tip of her nose. Her arms tightened around his neck and he was lost.

This time his mouth fastened on to hers, drinking in her sweetness. It seemed to flow through every part of his body, enriching his soul. He groaned softly, prising her lips apart and sliding his tongue into her mouth. He gentled her with his hands as he felt her shock and then, as he felt her relax against him, his tongue explored the soft inner regions of her mouth.

He was drowning in her, and memories of losing his brother and how this interlude had started came flooding into his mind. With a deep groan he pulled his mouth from hers and lowered her back on to the pillows. Taking comfort was one thing, but using Grace for his own selfish gratification was quite another.

Her bewilderment was reflected in the expression on her face. She was way out of her depth and he needed to make it clear that he wouldn't take advantage of her. *He wouldn't*! He repeated the words silently in his brain, until he managed to convince himself that he could be trusted with her obvious innocence.

She opened her mouth to speak, but he put his fingers against her lips. 'Don't say anything, Gracie. Neither of us is in very good shape at present and we…I…allowed myself to be carried away by the strength of my emotions. It won't happen again.'

Her head still felt fuzzy as Grace sifted through his words, still trying to understand her own reaction to the events which had taken place. 'It won't happen again' seemed to reverberate through her skull, and in the little reasoning which her tired brain could come up with – one fact stood out in neon lights. She wanted it to happen again.

chapter eight

The following morning Grace went about her tasks marvelling at how normal everything seemed after the rather tumultuous happenings of the previous day.

Nick had left her in the darkened room with strict instructions to rest, seemingly able to completely erase from his mind his short passionate outburst. He had insisted on doing all the work and the baby minding for the rest of the day and refused to let her get up, even heating the casserole and bringing her tea to her on a tray.

The shivers that pervaded her body every time she thought of his intimate kisses and the strength of his arms assured Grace that she was far from forgetting the experience and when she remembered her eager responses her face burned with embarrassment.

At least the previous evening's long rest had ensured that her physical strength had returned and her headache had gone, allowing Nick to go to the factory. He had gone quite early leaving Grace with the distinct feeling that he was glad to put some distance between them.

The more she tried to understand what had happened between them the more confused she became. Nick had blamed their emotions, but exactly what emotions was he targeting? He obviously didn't mean that his feelings were involved, which left only a physical attraction.

Grace had never felt that she was the sort of person to kick-start that magic chemistry that people spoke about and she imagined she was nothing like the type of woman who normally held any attraction for Nick.

The whole episode seemed to stem from her efforts to comfort him, but it hadn't been comfort he'd ultimately sought from her. Despite her naiveté she could recognise the signs of male arousal when she encountered them. She shivered. She was playing with fire. What had possessed her to respond the way she had and what would she have done if Nick had refused to stop?

'Oy! Those babies are setting up a chorus. Probably need a nappy change.'

Grace jumped as Dan's voice penetrated her thoughts. She became aware of the low-key whimpers which the twins had initiated and knew that in a few seconds the noise would develop into a full-blown roar.

'Where did you spring from?' She gave Dan a smile totally ignorant of the glazed look that came into his eyes.

'I arrived ten minutes ago, but I spent most of that time sending a suspicious looking character about his business.'

'How do you mean suspicious?' She couldn't quite fathom what he was talking about as they rarely had anyone call at the property.

'He was lurking at the gate and when I questioned him he asked who lived here. Who wants to know? I asked him. He then insisted he was looking for someone named Parker. There are no Parkers around here and I think he thought I'd tell him who did live here, but I'm not that green.'

Grace frowned wondering what the man had wanted. 'What did he do then?'

'He said he thought he had the wrong address and cleared off. You be sure you tell your old man about him.'

'I expect it's nothing to worry about,' Grace said, but Dan didn't agree.

'You tell Nick. You're a bit isolated here on this acreage, and I'm telling you that bloke looked damned suspicious.

Not from around here.' He paused taking the cap he always wore off his head and running an agitated hand through his hair. 'Foreigner,' he said, nodding his head as if he had just come to that conclusion. 'Dark complexioned. Evil looking face.'

Grace suppressed a shiver. She hoped Dan was exaggerating. The last thing she needed was someone in the vicinity who might pose a threat to her or the twins. What about Nick? She thought of his size and strength, and the vein of ruthlessness which she sensed ran deep within him. No, she couldn't imagine anyone being a threat to Nick.

The twins' protests had now increased by several decibels, so Grace left Dan to his morbid predictions and went to change the babies.

Later, when she made Dan a cup of tea, he didn't mention the stranger again and Grace decided it was probably a bit of a 'storm in a teacup'.

'How did you manage, yesterday?' Dan asked as he gulped a mouthful of scalding tea. 'I'd like to have seen Nick in the role of father for a change!'

'He managed very well, and he does help me you know, especially with the late feeds.' Grace hid a smile at the look of disappointment on Dan's face.

'It's the least he can do,' Dan said. 'I've met his kind before. They think that the only goal in life is to make money and establish themselves in their line of business. It's not right. A man should be there for his wife and be prepared to share raising his children.'

Having said his piece Dan took another mouthful of tea and Grace decided it was time to tell him a few home truths.

'Dan, Nick is the twins' father, but he is not my husband.'

That piece of information went down like a lead balloon as Dan choked on his tea.

'Not married to you!' He choked again and Grace was pondering whether to clap him between the shoulders when he got his breath back.

'I knew it,' he announced. 'He's just the type to seduce young women and then leave them literally holding the baby. Babies!' he added for good measure.

'It wasn't like that,' Grace hastened to put matters right. 'They're not my babies.'

'Not yours...?' Dan put his cup down looking totally confused.

'Sam and Sally are my sister's babies. She died soon after they were born, leaving them in my care. I needed help, so I came to Nick and he offered us a home.'

It wasn't exactly the truth, but as Dan's opinion of Nick was lower than a snake's belly she decided to do what she could to improve matters.

'But, they are his?' Dan's eyes narrowed.

'Yes,' Grace stated firmly, her stomach doing a war dance as she confronted the realisation that Nick had, at no stage, accepted the twins as his. She nodded her head reinforcing her statement. The last thing she needed was to have Dan casting doubts on their parentage.

'I'm surprised that he acknowledged them,' Dan said, confirming the direction of his thoughts. 'Although Sam's the spitting image of him.'

'He's been very generous,' Grace said.

'Rubbish!' Dan retorted. 'If he'd been "very generous", he'd have been supporting them from the moment they were born.'

'He didn't know that they existed,' Grace explained.

'I'll bet he wanted proof!'

Realising that they were getting into dangerous territory,

Grace quickly decided to change the direction of the conversation.

'He accepts them now,' she said firmly. 'They've become part of his life,' she added, crossing her fingers under the table, hoping that by embellishing the truth she wasn't tempting fate.

Dan got up and helped himself to another cup of tea and Grace had a feeling the inquisition wasn't over. She picked up her own cup and sipped the now lukewarm brew.

'So where do you fit in?' Dan asked as he lowered himself back on to the chair.

'I'm just here to fulfil my sister's dying wish, that I would look after her babies. After all, Nick has to have someone to care for them.'

'Convenient for him!'

Grace could see the way Dan's mind was working, and she could imagine the stories which would soon abound if she didn't clarify the situation.

'Dan, all that Nick and I share is the care of the babies. The only reason I live here with him, is to provide the home comforts that the twins require.'

'What about Nick's home comforts?' Dan asked bluntly.

'I'm happy to cook and clean for him,' Grace said. She paused a moment. 'Nothing else.'

'I don't like it.'

Grace couldn't hide her shock. 'Dan, it isn't anything to do with you!'

Dan shook his head. 'He's too much a man of the world for you. He'll take advantage of you.'

'No,' Grace said, remembering the previous evening. It had been Nick who had pulled back. When it came to the crunch Nick didn't really want her. 'No,' she repeated. 'He won't ever do that.'

'Why won't he?' Dan was like a dog with a bone.

Grace smiled. 'Because he doesn't fancy me. I'm not his type.' She stood up hoping to end the conversation, but tenacity seemed to be Dan's middle name.

'Doesn't fancy you?' He exclaimed, pushing his cup and saucer away as he stood up.

Grace, unsure whether to feel flattered or flustered at the astonishment in his tone, was relieved when he turned away.

But, he quickly swung around, clearly determined to have the last word. 'Maybe you aren't his type, Grace, but my guess is he'd be happy to try something new. So, you tread carefully and remember that if you need help, I'm always available.'

As Dan went back to work, she hoped that she'd done the right thing in telling him the truth. He'd probably have found out anyway, of course, but his defensive attitude bothered her a bit. Although she suspected, from his caring attitude towards the twins, that he was just protective by nature.

She wondered what he would think if he'd realised that she had almost brought about her own downfall? It was just as well that Nick had exercised some control. But the fact that he had only reinforced her belief that he wasn't really attracted to her – and that the thought of making love to her didn't really turn him on.

Nick rolled his chair back from the computer. A large window had been cut in the thick wall of the old reservoir, revealing a spectacular view of the valley below. He might as well have been casting his eye over a rubbish dump. He couldn't stop thinking of Grace and what it would have been like to make love to her.

Even thinking about it caused his body to react and he hastily propelled his chair back to the computer, where he could keep certain portions of his anatomy hidden under the desk.

Thank God he had kept his head last night! Although, with hindsight, he realised just how close he'd been to losing control. She was so completely different from any women he'd bedded before – and there had been quite a few. But they'd been more than willing, and they'd always known that for him there was no commitment.

He put his elbows on his desk and dropped his head into his hands. Grace had been willing. That's what had made the episode so damned difficult to cope with. But, she obviously *hadn't* known what she was doing – or that she was instinctively expecting some sort of a commitment from him.

His thoughts whirled around relentlessly. Who knew what she expected? Maybe she really was trying to trap him into some kind of relationship? After all, she was Karen's sister – and Karen hadn't had too many scruples.

He couldn't prevent a deep groan as the memory of the sweetness of her response filled his mind and hardened his body.

'Headache?'

His head jerked up. He hadn't heard the young woman come into his office. She was one of the factory staff, dark and sultry, and if he wasn't mistaken – and he usually wasn't – she would be readily available. One thing he'd learned from his problems with Karen, was never to mix business with pleasure, and he'd always made certain that he never messed with women whom he worked with. So, he gave her a cool appraisal before answering.

'Just the usual state of exhaustion after a night playing nursemaid to the twins.'

'Twins! You've got twins?'

If he'd said he had leprosy, it couldn't have had a more

desirable effect. Whatever she'd come for, she didn't bother staying to explain what it was, but swiftly took off like the proverbial rocket.

Nick leaned back in his chair, a smile spreading across his face. It would appear that having twins definitely lowered his appeal for the opposite sex!

The smile faded as he realised that his protection was a two-edged sword. Becoming a family man was fine when it suited him, but it also placed restrictions on his life which he hadn't even begun to think about.

He'd been his own man for so long, taking off across the world when the mood took him. Drifting in and out of shallow relationships. Becoming a parent was something he'd never contemplated and marriage was definitely not on his agenda.

As he mentally reinforced these facts, Nick realised that as far as most people were concerned, his attitude would be regarded as selfish and self-centred. But then, most people didn't know the reasons behind those rock-solid decisions.

If successful parenting was something one learned from one's parents, along with life's other lessons, then he hadn't exactly had perfect role models. The same could be said for learning the skills to maintain a happy marriage. His thoughts turned to his Uncle Will. He *had* been a role model, although he hadn't been married and he hadn't had any children.

Nick stood up and wandered over to the window. He'd really stuffed up. Whether he wanted children or not he had them now, and along with the children came Grace, which brought his thoughts back in a neat circle to where they had started.

It had been a wasted day, Nick decided, as he drove up the

track to the farmhouse. When he hadn't been lusting after Grace, he'd been chastising himself for letting time pass without making an effort to establish the twins' true parentage.

Normally he was a man of action and couldn't abide letting things drag on. He pulled up and slammed the car door shut. While he was on the subject of things dragging on, it looked as if he'd have to light a fire under Dan and Company and get the renovations finished. The final stages seemed to be taking forever and whenever he decided to check, Dan seemed to be drinking tea with Grace or nursing one of the babies.

He strode up the steps and into the lounge in time to witness Dan giving Sally a bottle and carrying on a ridiculous conversation that he was convinced no one understood.

'I'll do that,' he said slinging his briefcase into a corner. 'For God's sake – do what you're paid to do and finish renovating the damn house.'

Dan opened his mouth and shut it again. Silently handing Sally over he left the room.

Grace appeared in the doorway with Sam. 'I heard that,' she said. 'Do you *have* to be so rude? Or so aggressive? Dan is a real help to me and I don't need you to upset him.'

'He's an interfering busy-body,' Nick said. 'He had the cheek to tell me I didn't appreciate my wife.'

Grace bit back a grin. 'You should have told him that you didn't have a wife.'

Nick looked at her with narrowed eyes. 'Perhaps I did.'

'No,' Grace said. 'You didn't do that, because I had to explain our situation to him, this morning.'

'Over a pot of tea, no doubt,' Nick retorted grimly, trying to suppress both his anger and the unexpectedly strange, strong feeling that he would have preferred Dan to continue believing that he and Grace were married. 'He probably thinks we sleep together, anyway,' he added bluntly.

'No, he doesn't. I told him I was here to mind the babies. Nothing else.'

'If he believes that, he probably believes in fairies at the bottom of the garden!'

Grace hoisted Sam up on to her shoulder. 'Why shouldn't he believe it,' she demanded. 'Just because I share your house, there's no reason why I should have to share your bed.'

'You were damn close to sharing my bed yesterday!'

A moment later he saw the colour drain from her face, and felt like pig swill. What could he say? He didn't intentionally set out to hurt her, but his emotions were still coloured by frustration. He was wondering how to retrieve the situation, when the colour returned to her face and she let him have it with both barrels.

'You listen to me, Nicholas Best. What I offered you yesterday was sympathy – nothing else! Just because you think that every time a female touches you, it's an invitation to full blown sex – is your problem, not mine!'

She paused to draw breath and hoist Sam higher up on her shoulder. And then, for someone whose whole life was based on truth and goodness, she told the most outrageous lie of her life.

'If you think that I would have allowed you to make love to me, then you're living in a fool's paradise. I don't fancy you and, if you're honest with yourself, you'll admit that you don't fancy me.'

Nick opened his mouth to say something, when she floored him with another barrage. 'If you're suffering from an overdose of sexual frustration, then I suggest that you do something about it. There's plenty of hard physical work you can use to dampen your ardour. But, if that doesn't work, then you'll have to find someone and pay for the privilege.'

Pay for the privilege? The words reverberated around Nick's brain as she flounced out, with Sam still lying across her shoulder like a sack of potatoes. That was something he'd never had to do – and he sure as hell wasn't about to start now!

Nick dragged his thoughts back to the task of feeding Sally. She seemed uninterested in her bottle and he raised her up for a moment. She looked solemnly at him as if assessing his attraction for the opposite sex, before burping loudly and turning her head away.

Nick sighed. He could have sworn Grace was with him every inch of the way last night – but who knows what would have happened further down the track? She'd said that she didn't fancy him and she'd sounded convincing. He thought of the way she and Dan laughed together and their obvious companionship. Maybe she fancied Dan…?

It had been a bit like walking on eggshells, Grace thought, as she reviewed the past few days. She and Nick had managed to live together harmoniously, even sharing the ten o'clock feed, but their conversation had been almost non-existent and she'd caught Nick looking at her strangely a couple of times.

The lie she had told weighed on her conscience. She'd been more than ready to make love with Nick. That fact bothered her too. All her life, she had adhered to strong ideals and principles. They were perhaps a bit outdated, but she had seen the devastation which Karen had brought about with her wild ways, and had decided not to tread down that path.

Inevitably, selfishness and total disregard for other

people's feelings brought about unhappiness and problems. The twins were living proof of that. Not that she regarded them as a problem, Grace fiercely assured herself. They were and always would be the centre of her existence.

As if to prove to herself that her life revolved around the twins, Grace worked harder than ever. The room the twins were to occupy was finished and she organised their furniture, cleaned the windows until they sparkled and hung new curtains.

'You look exhausted,' Nick said as they shared the meal she had cooked. 'You don't want to lose any more weight.'

'Thank you for boosting my morale,' Grace said waspishly.

'It's not your morale I'm worried about,' Nick said. 'It's your health.'

Grace stood up thrusting her hair back from her face. 'You don't need to worry. I'm not about to take to my bed and leave you literally holding the babies again.'

Nick was temporarily distracted by her gesture of brushing back her hair. It had grown a little in the short time she had been living with him, and as he had suspected the thick lustrous curls provided a lovely frame for her classical features. He shook his head to dispel the direction his thoughts were taking.

'I didn't think that you were, but you need help around the house. I don't know why I took so long to realise it.'

'I can manage,' Grace said stubbornly.

'I know that you can manage,' Nick said, 'but you get no time to yourself.'

'I've had help at times from Dan,' Grace pointed out.

Nick flashed her an exasperated look. 'Yes, at the expense of the renovations.'

'They're almost finished,' Grace said.

Nick nodded thinking that at last he'd get rid of the

pesky Dan. Damn paragon always helping out with the twins and criticising Nick's performance as a father. At least he'd dropped the snide remarks about husbands.

'Perhaps if you check the local paper you'll find someone to help both with the housework and minding the twins. Be sure and ask for references.'

Grace bit her lip. She could do with the help, but it put her deeper into his debt and he still hadn't said if he had managed to prove that the twins were his although she didn't doubt that she would have heard about it if he'd proved they weren't.

Dan came to the rescue with the household help. His cousin was a qualified nanny and had no objection to doing some housework. He brought her to meet Grace and the twins just before he finished off the last of the work on the house.

'This is Lucy,' he announced to Grace, thrusting forward a tall, attractive lass with long straight brown hair.

Grace decided on the spot to give Lucy the job. She had the same affinity with the twins that Dan had and from what she knew about Dan and his extended family they were well thought of by everyone in the district. Mentally Grace excluded Nick from that list of supporters. More and more he seemed to resent Dan and perhaps it was as well that Lucy had a different surname.

They were sharing the last feed of the day when Grace broached the subject of the household help. She told Nick about Lucy, carefully leaving out her relationship to Dan.

'She's a qualified nanny,' she explained.

'Great,' Nick said sitting Sam up on his lap.

'Well yes,' Grace agreed, 'but, that means we…you'll have to pay her a bit more.'

Nick shrugged that off. 'The main thing is to get

someone reliable. She did have references?'

'Yes, but…'

'But what?' Nick said, his eyes narrowing at her embarrassment. 'Aren't you sure about her?'

'Yes, it's not that.'

'What is it then? Stop pussy footing around and spit out whatever it is that's bugging you.'

'It's the money,' Grace blurted out.

'Forget the damned money,' Nick said taking one of Sam's small hands in his and spreading his little fingers out on his large palm.

'But, you're paying so much in support of the twins and I know you don't entirely believe that they belong to you.'

Nick didn't say anything at all. He was staring fascinated at Sam's fingers. He sat there for several minutes before he finally stood up with Sam in his arms.

He began to walk from the room, presumably intending to put Sam into his cot. He paused in the doorway. 'What I believe isn't important,' he said. 'The future and well being of the twins is all that matters.'

chapter nine

Grace sat holding Sally. There was no doubt in her mind that Nick was becoming attached to the twins and he'd even extended that attachment to Sam, spending more time with him than he had previously. He certainly had their well being at heart, but what if they weren't his? She shook her head. That wasn't an option. She believed Karen, and why would she lie about their father?

Uneasily Grace tried to banish the thoughts that flashed through her mind. What if Karen had selected Nick as the father because he was wealthy? What if she wasn't sure who was the father? Grace sighed. Karen's morals had certainly been suspect and her lifestyle bordering on decadent.

Wearily Grace rose to her feet and carried Sally into the bedroom. Sometimes it all became too much and she felt bowed down with the insecurity of her position. Nick was standing over Sam's cot, a bemused look on his face. As she glanced from one to the other Grace felt reassured. Dan was right. Sam was the image of Nick.

She tucked Sally in and left Nick beside Sam's cot. He put out his hand and Sam clutched Nick's little finger in his fist.

As she made herself a hot drink, Grace offered up a silent prayer. There seemed to be some sort of bonding going on between Nick and Sam. Not before time, she thought, remembering how he had avoided Sam in the early days of their arrival.

Now that she knew of the tragic loss of Nick's younger

brother she could understand his attitude especially if there was also a physical resemblance between Sam and the Sam who had been killed. Maybe one day Nick would tell her what actually happened, but it would have to be when he felt ready and he obviously didn't feel that way at the moment.

Surfacing from a deep sleep, Grace lay and listened to the birds. The variety was endless. Lorikeets, corellas, magpies and honeyeaters of all kinds. Their songs blended into the background, even the screeches of the parrots lending their own particular music. She realised that for the first time in months she felt relaxed.

The twins were seven months old now and sleeping well at night. The renovations were finished and, apart from the strong smell of fresh paint, the house was a dream to live in with its new kitchen, bathroom and larger rooms.

As each room was finished, Nick had bought new furniture and also unearthed some of the treasures which he'd brought back from his travels. He was unpacking a large box in the lounge when Grace finally joined him, fresh from her shower.

He paused for a moment as she stood before him, her hair in damp curls around her face, her skin fresh and glowing.

'Twins?' he asked.

'Sleeping in, this morning,' Grace said with a smile. 'I hope it's a sign of things to come. They should cut out that ten o'clock feed soon too.'

Nick nodded and returned to his unpacking, removing several layers of tissue paper before carefully lifting out a shimmering crystal bowl.

'Oh, that's absolutely beautiful!' Grace exclaimed. It was a large bowl and its multi-faceted surface glowed and shimmered in the sunlight, streaming in through the window.

'Waterford Crystal,' Nick said. 'It belonged to my Uncle Will. Sort of a family heirloom.'

He placed the bowl carefully on a sturdy carved wooden table, and Grace watched as he stood back and admired it. She was surprised at his reaction. Nick didn't seem to be particularly attached to material things.

Grace shivered. At times she wondered if there was anyone in his life he felt deeply about. There was no denying his care and consideration towards her and the twins, but that didn't mean his feelings were deeply involved.

'We'll have to treasure it,' Grace said and then blushed as she realised she was speaking as if they were a couple.

'Yeah!' Nick hadn't noticed her discomfort as he picked up the empty box and the paper and left the room.

Grace stood for a long time looking at the bowl. It would be a mixed blessing she thought. On one hand she was happy to see that Nick treasured something in his life, even if it was inanimate. On the other hand, she would have nightmares when the twins became mobile.

She turned away and her shoulders slumped. Who knows where they'd be when the twins became mobile? She looked at the bowl again and wished that it was a crystal ball. At least she'd know what lay ahead of her, instead of this terrible uncertainty. So much for her period of relaxation. It must have lasted all of thirty minutes.

'The beach!' If Nick had suggested going to the moon, Grace couldn't have been more surprised.

'Yes, the beach.' The exasperation was barely contained as Nick repeated himself. 'You know. Surf, sand, sun. All that healthy stuff that we never seem to indulge in.'

And whose fault's that? Grace thought. Apart from helping with the twins' feeds, and of course paying for help, Nick seemed loath to spend extra time with her or the twins. The factory was certainly up and running, but it still had the major call on Nick's time.

Just gathering together the necessary items for a couple of hours at the beach seemed a major operation. As Nick stuffed the last of the items into the Range Rover, Grace thought it would be easier to stay home.

No, that wasn't fair to the twins, she chided herself, as she buckled up her seat belt. They were growing up and taking an interest in their surroundings and a sojourn at the beach would be just what they needed.

As Nick slammed the door on the mountain of paraphernalia required for the day's outing, he wondered if he needed his head examined. Guilt gnawed at him every time he looked at Grace and her reed thin figure. Which was why he'd suggested the day's outing, so that she could have some rest and relaxation.

He shook his head as he opened the driver's door. Fat lot he knew about babies and relaxation! Going on a day's excursion was clearly like planning a battle campaign. Once again, the serious inroads that having a family made on one's normal existence, hit him amidships. Glumly, he wondered if his life would ever be normal again? Whatever normal was.

He glanced at Grace as she relaxed back in her seat, her eyes closed. Firing up the engine he gave himself a silent pep talk. She had been a victim of circumstances, some of which he was indirectly responsible for, and yet she never complained. He decided to make her day one to remember, little realising what a day it would turn out to be.

Nick whistled softly as he drove along the busy highway and Grace opened her eyes, praying that his relaxed attitude was a sign of contentment. If only he would give some sort of indication that he intended keeping the twins permanently, it would ease her mind tremendously. And, if he did so, would he keep her on too – and in what capacity?

It was difficult to believe that they'd been with him for weeks, and yet he still hadn't discussed the question of Sally and Sam's parentage. Of course, the renovations and establishing his factory had demanded a great deal of his time, but considering the impact fatherhood was making on his life, she thought that he would have wanted to resolve the issue.

A long sigh escaped her lips. The insecurity of her position did nothing for her nervous system. But, if she instigated a discussion, it might well precipitate a situation which she'd find even harder to deal with. Her problems were endless. She just seemed to be managing to come to grips with difficulty, when another reared its ugly head.

'That was a heartfelt sigh,' Nick said. 'Want to tell me what's bothering you?'

'Not unless you've got a spare decade or so to listen,' she said.

He glanced at her in surprise. 'You can't have that many problems, Grace. I know Karen lumbered you with the twins, but you manage them really well.'

Grace winced at the word 'lumbered'. Was that how he felt? It didn't do anything to enhance her sense of security.

'There's nothing else is there?' He paused and she noticed his strong tanned hands clench tightly on to the steering wheel. 'It's not Dan is it? He hasn't been coming on to you has he?' He hit the wheel with one hand. 'Because if he has I'll…'

'It's nothing to do with Dan.' She bit her tongue. What if Dan had shown an interest in her? It had nothing to do with Nick. Not unless he was scared she would clear off and leave him to cope with the twins.

Grace let her breath ease out during the uncomfortable silence, hoping the third degree was over. It wasn't.

'You've never told me what you were doing when Karen's problems surfaced,' he said. 'You said you were a teacher so I presume you were teaching.'

Her thoughts went into complete disarray and Grace was trying to cobble them into some sort of order and come up with a reasonable explanation when fate intervened.

The loud bang reverberated through the air and Grace jumped in her seat, giving a short scream of alarm as Nick fought to keep control of the vehicle. His strength and deadly calm was the only thing between them and a fatal accident. When he pulled over to the side of the road Grace slumped in her seat, before stiffening and whipping around to check the twins. They were lying back in their safety seats, none the worse for their ordeal.

'What was it,' she asked. 'Did a tyre blow out?'

'No!' Nick looked grim as he got out of the car, hurling a terse, 'Don't move!' in her direction. he ran back looking up as he did and Grace put her head out of the window.

They had travelled under an overhead bridge. Nick was now running back towards the bridge, his eyes scanning the high walkway as he ran. There was no one there. However, as the pieces of the puzzle fell into place, Grace realised that whatever it was which had hit the front of their car, it had probably been thrown down from the bridge.

It was a mercy the windscreen had escaped. Grace shuddered as she thought of the consequences of Nick having to drive virtually blind. Through the wide front glass she could see a large indentation in the bonnet of the car.

Nick appeared at her window. 'No one there, but it's obvious that someone hurled a rock at our vehicle.' He examined the damage to the car and shook his head. 'A large rock if I'm not mistaken. We were lucky not to be killed.'

'But…' It was all unbelievable to Grace. As she thought of the two beautiful babies in the back she felt sick. 'How could anyone harm two little children?'

Nick shook his head. 'If, as I suspect, it was some loutish kids, then they obviously didn't think the consequences through.'

'But they must have known it would cause an accident.' The tremor in her voice alerted Nick to the shock she had sustained, and he opened her door and pulled her into his arms. For a few moments he just held her, glancing back at the twins to reassure himself that they hadn't suffered any injuries.

'As I said, Gracie, kids don't always think these things through. There's been a couple of incidents like this lately and one driver was badly hurt.'

Grace lay against his chest. Even now he was breathing heavily. She wasn't the only one who was shocked. She drew back a little. 'What should we do?'

'Drive on and call in to the nearest police station. If you feel up to it, we might as well keep going to the beach. Apart from the damage to the bodywork, it looks as though the car is still OK to drive.'

It was the last thing Grace felt like doing, but perhaps it was better to concentrate on going somewhere…anywhere that might take their minds off the near-miss they'd just experienced.

The police station was only small, but the middle-aged policeman took in the situation at a glance, putting the electric kettle on and making them a cup of tea.

'We've had a couple of reports like this,' he told them.

'We view the whole thing very seriously. If it's not stopped there'll be a fatal accident.' He ran a fatherly eye over the twins lying on a rug on the floor. 'God knows what kind of upbringing results in kids trying to run someone off the road, but there is a real need for education on road safety both for parents and children.'

After reassuring them that there would be regular police patrols in the area until the culprits were caught, he saw them out to their car and suggested they try to put the whole unpleasant incident behind them.

'That's not to say I won't be in touch, because I'll keep you posted on any progress we make,' he told Nick as he closed the door of their car and waved them off.

As they pulled into the parking area near the beach, Grace looked out towards the sand and the sea. It all looked so normal, the sand dotted with people soaking up the sun, and the sea liberally sprinkled with swimmers waiting for a suitable wave to surf. She shivered as she realised how lucky they were to be there and not in some hospital ward – or worse.

'Cold?' Nick asked, as they left the car and walked down on to the sand, each carrying a baby.

'No. Just trying to come to grips with the events of the last hour or so.'

'Try to put it behind you, Grace. Dwelling on what might have happened never helps.'

He was right, she told herself. She'd wasted far too much time going over her past life, her mistakes and her unrealistic ambitions.

Nick spread a brightly patterned cotton rug on the sand, laying the babies on it while he erected a large beach umbrella.

'I'll change into my swimming costume,' she said, picking up her bag and heading for the nearby change rooms. She glanced back to see Nick shedding his clothes, revealing the brief swimwear which he'd been wearing underneath.

It took only minutes to change and the large umbrella and bright rug made it easy to find Nick and the babies amongst the crowd. He was undressing the twins when she joined them clad in her neat black one-piece outfit. Nick looked up and paused for a moment and Grace felt as if she was under a microscope.

Two could play at that game. He was kneeling down to work the baby clothes off each squirming twin, and all she could see was his broad chest, sprinkled with black curly hair. His skin was deeply tanned and her lively imagination conjured up several scenarios as to where that tanning could have taken place.

Having stripped each child down to a nappy he quickly applied sun block. He stood up and hoisted Sally with him handing her to Grace. She almost dropped her. Nick's long legs, tanned, with a light covering of dark hair, fascinated her. Altogether he made an eye-boggling picture and Grace was ashamed at the uncontrollable hormonal surge that flooded her system.

Water, preferably cold, was the answer she felt sure. After all cold showers worked for men didn't they? She strode into the sea realising that she was entrapped at the edge. She could hardly take Sally in where they might both fall victim to a large wave, which had the potential to up-end them.

Nick joined her with Sam and after a while they took it in turns to sit with the twins on the beach under the umbrella while the other had a swim.

'You'll get well and truly cooked,' Nick said when they had finished their swim. 'I put baby sunscreen on the twins. Did you put any on when you changed?'

'No.' Grace bit her lip. How irresponsible could she get? She should have thought to put the sunscreen on the babies and as for herself, a creamy skinned redhead, protection from the sun should be a religion.

'Here.' Nick came and stood close to her with a bottle of sunscreen in his hand. She put out her hand, but he turned her around and began to apply the sunscreen to her back.

As his hands progressed downward over the backs of her legs Grace had to bite down on the moan that almost left her lips. The fact that his hands were roughened from hard work only added to the sensual experience.

When he turned her gently around again and started to stroke the creamy liquid on to her neck, arms and the front of her legs, Grace felt mindless with desire. She closed her eyes as he rubbed some cream on to her face.

In her mind the beach disappeared and they were lying together in a soft bed, their naked bodies intertwined as Nick stroked every part of her body.

'That should do you.'

Her eyes flew open as reality struck. What was wrong with her? She was fantasising about making love with Nick in the middle of a crowded beach.

'Are you all right?' Nick looked at her anxiously. 'You're not getting over heated are you?'

Grace bit back the hysterical laugh that threatened to erupt. Overheated. That was the understatement of the year. She was on fire for him. Little Gracie, always in control, never allowing her emotions to rule her head, saving herself for...for what? For someone who valued her, respected her and cherished her. There might be someone who fitted that criteria, but somehow she didn't think it was Nick.

While she struggled to dampen her erotic thoughts Nick

closed the cap on the sunscreen and handed her the bottle. He strode back into the water and she watched as his curly black head disappeared beneath the waves.

Grace shrugged as she watched him surface and swim strongly towards the breakers. No doubt he felt that having sun protected both her and the babies his obligations had been fulfilled and he could enjoy the surf. So much for her sex appeal. On a score of one to ten she probably hadn't even registered.

chapter ten

Nick revelled in the cool water. His mouth twisted in a wry grin. He'd be revelling for quite a while if the state of his male anatomy was any indication. Thank God Grace hadn't noticed his battle for control. Covering her with sunscreen had been sheer indulgence – and boy, had it backfired! The minute he'd started stroking her soft skin, he had known that he was in trouble. Deep trouble!

His mind focused on other trouble. The incident below the bridge. Perhaps children had been responsible, but there was a sinister feel about the whole episode which made his blood run cold.

He remembered the fury that had erupted in him when he'd finally got the vehicle under control. He'd felt angry in the past and had often felt like retaliation, but his feelings when he thought of what could have happened to Grace and the babies were murderous.

The bright green beach umbrella stood out against the background of yellow sand and he could see Grace playing with the twins. They were propped up against a blow up cushion and she was moving her hands in front of them. He knew she would be singing songs and doing the actions. He'd seen her doing it many times.

Perhaps it was her background in teaching that saw her making the most of every occasion to enhance their knowledge and enjoyment. There was no doubt in his mind that the twins' lives had been enriched by their enforced reliance on Grace. What about Grace's life?

As the cool water dampened his raging hormones Nick

wondered about Grace. What had she sacrificed to look after the twins? What did she see happening in her future and what part would he play in it?

He felt as if a chasm was opening beneath him and that he would fall into a bottomless void. He didn't plan too far into the future and he'd never planned that future around anyone but himself. His gaze drifted to the shore again. He couldn't walk away.

It was ages before he emerged and the sight of Grace, slim and curvaceous in her one-piece swimsuit, almost set him off again. He lowered his large frame on to the sand beside her.

'They look sleepy.' He nodded towards the twins.

'Yes. They'll be off the minute we get back into the car.'

He thought he detected a tremor in her voice and he had no doubt it was the thought of their return journey that was bothering her.

'Let's find somewhere to have lunch,' he suggested. 'You stay here with the twins until I stow all the gear and then we'll take them with us to a nearby cafe.'

They attracted quite a bit of attention as Nick pushed the double stroller containing the two babies. Grace hid a smile wondering what he was thinking. He was totally out of his environment and she doubted that he'd ever performed such a task before.

Guilt filtered through her amusement. 'Would you like me to push?'

'Not unless you want to develop arms like a Sumo wrestler,' he said. 'This pair must weigh a ton.'

'They're certainly thriving.' Grace ran a proud eye over the babies. Sam was a real little bruiser and Sally wasn't far behind him. They were nothing alike with Sally's red hair a startling contrast to Sam's jet-black thatch.

'This OK?' Nick indicated a busy cafe with outdoor tables overlooking the beach.

Grace nodded, 'It's fine.'

'You relax,' Nick said, parking the stroller beside one of the chairs. 'I'll go in and order.'

Grace subsided gratefully into the chair and watched the people passing by. They all looked so normal, but she knew from past experience that so-called normality often hid vast problems and unhappiness.

Take their own situation. To outsiders they probably looked like a loving family when in fact they were just a fractured group trying to sort out a host of problems.

She thought of Nick's words. 'You relax,' he'd said. Her thoughts flew back to their first encounter. Helping her to relax hadn't been high on his priority list then. He'd seemed more interested in lighting a fire under her nervous system.

Was he changing? Had he changed? She glanced at the babies and thought of the enormous changes they had made to her life. It wasn't possible that they hadn't had a drastic effect on Nick's life and... Yes! She could see subtle changes in his personality and she wondered if he had detected those changes himself.

'Whew! I think everybody and his dog had the same idea about coming to the beach.' Nick appeared with a laden tray and a slightly harassed expression.

'Toasted sandwiches, cake and coffee OK? Decaffeinated coffee,' he added.

'Lovely.' After the incident with the rock Grace had completely lost her appetite, but at the sight of the delicious food she felt hungry.

'What about those two?' Nick indicated the twins who were into solid food in a big way.

'I've got some pureed food for them,' Grace said.

They ate their lunch in a leisurely fashion, and Grace fed the babies.

'Feeling better?' Nick leaned back in his chair and looked at her through narrowed eyes.

'Yes.' For just a few moments Grace pretended that they were a loving family. After all Nick was behaving very much like a caring husband and father.

She gave a gentle sigh. He wouldn't relish the comparison. His care and concern was just that of one human being for another and by reading anything else into it she was only leaving herself open for heartache.

Pushing her empty plate away she stood up. 'Perhaps we should go.'

Nick stood up and took hold of the stroller. 'Sure. Sam and Sally are probably more than ready for a sleep.'

By the time they were strapped into their car seats the twins were nodding off. Nick folded up the stroller and shoved it into the back of the vehicle.

'It's certainly a major project taking that pair anywhere,' he commented.

He grinned as he spoke, but Grace wondered if he was feeling the restrictions that going anywhere with a ready-made family placed on him.

Guiltily she remembered her own reactions at times when going out seemed more trouble than it was worth. She had enjoyed the day though, except for the incident earlier.

Nick guided the big vehicle along the highway and she relaxed in her seat glimpsing the changing scenery as it flashed by. Sugarcane farms gave way to pine forests and in the distance she could see the oddly shaped mountains with aboriginal names.

It was all familiar country and she treasured it. She turned and smiled at Nick, but he was concentrating on driving. Her stomach turned over as she recognised the overhead bridge up above. Her hands clenched into fists and as they went under the bridge Nick took one of her hands in his large one and held it tightly.

They passed under without incident and Nick let go of her hand and returned his to the steering wheel. Grace relaxed back in her seat and let her eyes slide towards Nick. His face was grim and he appeared to be watching the road ahead.

Despite the hard-bitten exterior he presented to the outside world she knew now that he was sensitive to other people's feelings. There were depths to his personality that she still hadn't discovered and she knew there was still a great deal to learn about the real Nick Best. And she loved him. She smothered the gasp that almost escaped her lips as that realisation hit home. Her hands clenched again.

Nick turned a pair of near black eyes towards her. 'Relax, Gracie. It was a one-off incident. You're perfectly safe now.'

She glanced at him. His shoulders were huge, his face rugged, and that ridiculous lock of silver hair contrasting violently with the jet-black, slightly curly hair covering his head. He reminded her of some vagabond gypsy – and he absolutely screamed sex appeal!

Sex appeal. Grace clung to the words like a drowning man would to a life raft. That's all it was. A physical attraction.

'I'm not afraid,' she said. She lay back in her seat and closed her eyes. No, not afraid. Terrified. Her life was complicated enough without falling in love with the devil himself. It's a physical attraction she chanted inside her head. That she could deal with. The twins were the living testimony of what happened when people gave in to physical temptation.

Nick apparently accepted her statement at face value and they completed their journey in silence, each steeped in their own thoughts. Grace gave a wry smile. If there was one thing she was sure of it was that Nick's thoughts were unlikely to run along the same lines as hers.

As soon as they reached home they unpacked the vehicle and successfully transferred the twins to their cots to continue sleeping.

Nick's thoughts were in turmoil. He rammed an old hat on his head and left by the back door. He headed for the fence-line and stood under a stand of trees as he leaned on the wooden post.

He couldn't keep evading the issue. His thoughts turned to his Uncle Will and the advice he'd drummed into him from childhood. Marriage was for people who wanted to play 'happy families'. That was a laugh. How many families were really happy? Dropping his head in his hands Nick thrust away the few happy memories of his childhood he had. The few times his mother had shown him affection. It was almost as if she had been afraid to love him. He shuddered. Was that how he felt about little Sam?

Memories came thick and fast now. His years at boarding school, paid for by Uncle Will. He'd been happy enough there away from his father's silent criticism.

Holidays more often than not spent with his uncle. He'd been the envy of classmates with overseas trips and a rich uncle hovering in the background. Engineering, following in his uncle's footsteps, had been a natural choice and his university education further alienated him from his parents, who were left with the family farm and only Sam to take over as they got older. But Sam's only interest had been in having a good time and that had led him into trouble.

There'd been the money of course. He sent it regularly

to his father, now a widower, to help maintain the farm. Nick thought about Uncle Will's legacy. It had made him a very wealthy man, but it was the legacy of his virtual upbringing that had the most profound effect.

Uncle Will had never married and urged Nick to follow the same path. Women only stuff things up he'd declared, and children, they can make or break a marriage. Don't bother with either he'd counselled.

Nick drew his breath in sharply. Uncle Will had bothered with him and he'd been a child when his uncle had taken him under his wing, so in a way he hadn't been true to his own philosophy. His thoughts winged back over the years. Will had never made him feel a liability and as he had grown to adulthood they had become even closer.

Nick shrugged his shoulders looking skywards. What now? The children were a fact of life and as long as Grace stayed to look after them he felt a responsibility towards her. Legally he mightn't be bound to either, but morally he felt about as hog tied as a man could feel.

As he wandered around his property he noticed the dry grass and thick stands of gum trees. They needed rain and the grass needed mowing again. Another commitment, but hadn't he known that when he bought the five-acre lot? The factory was another permanent factor in his life. He realised he'd unconsciously wandered from the footloose and fancy-free path when he settled in the area and started up his business.

Maybe there was more of his father in him than he realised. He shivered. His father had let him down. Oh sure, his father had never shown him any malice, but then he'd shown him little emotion of any kind.

Clenching his fists at his side he made a vow that if he was going to embrace fatherhood whether it be willingly or not he would be a good father. No matter what the circumstances he would never allow his children to suffer the guilt and trauma that he had endured.

Grace watched as Nick began to walk back towards the house. He was unhappy. Depressed even. She longed to help him, but he wouldn't talk about his background. There was a barrier around him that she couldn't penetrate. It made her feel very much the household help and cancelled out any of the togetherness which she'd felt today on the beach.

Despite the lines of demarcation that Nick adhered to they had more in common than he was prepared to acknowledge. Grace mentally ticked off the events that coloured both their lives. They had both lost a sibling. They shared a mutual bond with the twins' future held in their hands. Nick was obviously being tormented by past experiences that had left deep scars. She sucked in her breath. Perhaps it wasn't so much past experiences, but the present and future that was causing his depression.

Grace chewed her lip as she considered her own past. Scarred was probably too strong a word to describe her situation. Certainly she had suffered a loss of self-esteem, confidence, and the ability to map out her future. She shrugged. It scarcely mattered now. Her future had been taken out of her hands when Karen died and she had assumed responsibility for the twins.

Monday morning came around quickly and as she stood at the kitchen window Grace felt a twinge of guilt. Dan's white utility bumped up the track bringing Lucy to begin her day's work helping with the twins and the housework. As Nick always left early he didn't realise that Lucy was Dan's cousin or that Dan ferried her to the farmhouse each day.

Grace heard the car doors slam and her guilt rose a notch

or two. It wasn't as if Dan let Lucy off and then went on to his worksite. He always came in and spent a few minutes with the twins.

'You OK?' Dan's tousled head appeared around the kitchen door.

'Yes, of course.' Grace managed a bright smile. The last thing she needed was Dan wearing his protector's hat. That he didn't consider her living arrangements a safe environment was obvious and if he had known about their near miss under the bridge yesterday he would have gone into orbit.

'You look pale,' Dan said, giving her a searching glance.

'Redheads always look pale,' she said. 'Won't you be late for work?'

'Doesn't matter when I'm running the show,' Dan said.

'Yes it does.' Lucy came into the kitchen clutching Sally under one arm. 'You should set a good example.'

Grace heaved a sigh of relief when Dan took himself off grumbling about knowing when he wasn't wanted.

'He's got the hots for you,' Lucy announced and laughed as Grace made a grab for the cup she dropped.

'He's just a nice person who cares about people,' Grace insisted.

'Oh, he's a very nice person,' Lucy said, adding with a cheeky grin, 'a very nice person with the hots for you.'

Grace shook her head and went to make the beds. It was the last thing she needed to hear. Nick mightn't have any interest in her, but his reaction to Dan was negative to say the least. Thinking about that Grace wondered just what it was that made Nick so anti-Dan. He couldn't be jealous. Could he?

Brutal honesty forced Grace to acknowledge that it wouldn't be jealousy that fired Nick up where Dan was concerned. Possession maybe. He may not have admitted parentage where the twins were concerned, but he wasn't sharing them with anyone else at this stage and he seemed to regard Grace as part of the package.

'I'll take the twins for a walk down the track.' Lucy appeared in the doorway with the twins in the double stroller.

Grace walked to the door with Lucy and helped her negotiate the steps with the babies in the buggy. It was another hot dry day and Grace was glad that Lucy and the twins were wearing hats.

'Better stick to the shady areas,' Grace suggested, although she knew Lucy was totally reliable and sensible. No way would she put the babies at risk.

'Sure,' Lucy nodded. 'I just think they need a bit of healthy outside air every day, although in this heat the benefit to their health is debatable.'

Grace went back up the steps and turned in the doorway to look out over the property. The long grass was brown now from lack of water and some of the less hardy trees were dying. The sheen of water sparkling in the sun- shine drew her eyes to the dam and she was relieved to note that the water level was still quite high. She remembered Nick saying that he intended organising some kind of watering system from the dam when he got the property landscaped.

It really was too hot for walking, even around the prop- erty, and when Lucy re-appeared at the door in a short time Grace helped her unbuckle the twins and carry them into the house.

'I think cool drinks all around are the go,' Grace said, pouring iced orange juice for herself and Lucy and cool boiled water for the twins.

'That really hit the spot,' Lucy said, putting her glass on the table as she helped the twins manipulate their new feeding cups. 'Who's the dark guy hanging around next door?'

'Next door?' Grace thought for a moment. 'We don't see much of our neighbours because of the size of the properties. I thought Nick said the neighbours were away.'

Lucy shrugged. 'He was down at their front gate near the mailbox. He looked away when I got close.'

Grace chewed her lip. 'I don't know the neighbours so he probably didn't think it necessary to say anything.' She felt a twinge of uneasiness. The little contact she'd had with people living in the area had been pleasant and the local folk had gone out of their way to be friendly.

Keeping up with the demands of the twins didn't leave much time for speculation, but every now and then Grace's thoughts turned to the strange man. She remembered Dan saying something about a strange man asking questions and she hadn't heeded his advice to tell Nick about it. Why would someone be watching the house or her? Unless...

Grace drew in a breath as a thought slid into her mind. Was Nick investigating the twins' background? Perhaps the man was a private investigator. It didn't make sense. He wouldn't be investigating the area where Nick lived. Nick would have filled him in on that aspect.

The day seemed to fly by and Grace was still worrying at the problem when Dan arrived to collect Lucy. Telling Dan wasn't an option, as she hadn't taken his advice earlier.

Lucy seemed to take forever to get her gear together and Dan took the opportunity to play with the twins. They all heard the Rover's engine cut out and three heads swung towards the door.

It couldn't be Nick, Grace thought. He never came home this early. She was still living in a fool's paradise when he marched through the door.

'What the hell...?' The sight of Dan holding Sam

seemed to temporarily rob him of speech.

'Just called to collect Lucy,' Dan threw into the charged atmosphere.

'Lucy? You know Lucy?' Nick's head swivelled in Grace's direction and she could feel the silent inquisition.

'Of course I know her,' Dan said. 'She's my cousin.'

'Of course she is,' Nick said still looking at Grace. If looks could incinerate, she knew she would be a little pile of white-hot ash.

'You're early,' Grace said, compounding her guilt.

'Obviously,' Nick said. 'I'm meeting the man who's installing the fire pump.'

'Oh!' The lines of communication left a lot to be desired, but Grace knew that she had engineered her own downfall and that she would hear about it later.

'We'll be off,' Dan said. He looked at Nick and obviously not liking what he saw he turned to Grace and deposited Sam in her arms. He had swept Lucy up and thrust her into the utility before anything else was said and as they rattled down the driveway they passed the truck with the fire pump heading towards the house.

Nick took a step towards Grace and she lifted Sam high in her arms shielding her face. He swung away from her in disgust and went out the back door as the truck pulled up with a squeal of brakes.

The unloading and installation of the fire pump gave Grace time to prepare for a showdown with Nick. She heard him come in and head for the shower as she got the twins ready for bed. By the time she had prepared tea she felt more settled. Perhaps he wouldn't be angry about her deception.

He wasn't angry. He was livid. He fired the first salvo as he strode into the kitchen. 'You deliberately kept from me the information that Lucy was Dan's cousin. You knew

I wouldn't have approved her as a nanny.'

'Which would have been a mistake,' Grace threw at him. 'Lucy is an excellent nanny, and her competence has nothing to do with Dan.'

'I'm not talking about Lucy's ability,' Nick roared. 'It's the appendage attached to her that I object to. You must have known that Dan would find an excuse to hang around here. Getting you to employ his cousin must have been a gift from heaven.'

'I didn't realise when I employed Lucy that she was dependent on Dan for transport.'

'Did you ask?'

Grace shook her head.

'No. I didn't think so.' Nick's eyes narrowed. 'I suppose it gives you a buzz to have a male drooling over you. Perhaps you're not so different from your sister after all.'

Grace took a step close to him and thrust out her chin. 'Perhaps I'm not,' she said.

She heard his sharp intake of breath. 'So there is something going on between you and Dan.'

'No, there is not. Dan and Lucy are good people and I appreciate the help they give me. None of us has an ulterior motive and if you weren't so prepared to see the worst in everyone you'd realise that.'

'Oh, so it's all my fault now.' Nick threw up his hands in exasperation. 'Sometimes I wonder if you're for real, Grace. How you can stand there and deny that Dan has no interest in you leaves me speechless.'

'He hasn't.' The minute the words had left her mouth Grace remembered Lucy's claim about Dan having the 'hots' for her. She bit down on her bottom lip. He was always around and he resented the fact that she shared a house with Nick.

Nick's eyes honed in on hers as he watched the changing

expressions on her face. 'Having doubts?' he slipped in.

'No, of course not. Besides…'

'Besides what?'

It was a bit like the Spanish Inquisition and Grace wasn't even sure herself what she was going to say. 'It isn't as if I give him any encouragement. I wouldn't do that when…'

'When you know that starting a relationship with someone would make your position here very tenuous.'

She almost laughed at his aggressive stance. Starting a relationship with Dan couldn't be further from her mind. Not when she loved Nick totally.

He was laying down the ground rules. Not that she wasn't instinctively aware of them. There were always rules, it seemed, governing her life and her choices. It wasn't the first time she felt stifled by them and it wasn't the first time she'd rebelled. Even the man she loved wasn't going to bind her in silken threads.

'My position isn't the only one that's tenuous,' she said. 'If I walked out of here tomorrow you'd have difficulty coping.'

'Is that so? What about the redoubtable Dan and his cousin Lucy? Haven't you just insisted their sole aim in life is to provide care for the twins? Wouldn't they be ready to step into the breach?'

Tears sprang to her eyes. He didn't need her. He certainly didn't love her and it seemed as if he didn't care about her. Her insides felt as if they were being sliced to ribbons, but each day she was becoming more battle hardened and she wasn't about to let him score an easy victory.

She threw her head back and sent him a searing look. 'I'm sure with your influence and money you can provide twenty four hour care for the twins, but they need more than that. They need love and trust.'

Nick opened his mouth to speak, but she was too quick

for him. 'You've never heard of the word love and I realise now that the trust I had in you was severely misplaced.'

As she left the room she kept her face averted. He would never know the degree of hurt he had inflicted. She closed the door without a backward glance totally unaware that the pain and hurt she felt was mirrored in even greater depth on Nick's features.

chapter eleven

The kitchen chair creaked under Nick's weight as he sat down heavily, letting his head drop into his hands. What the hell did he care if she didn't trust him? He was living proof that survival was entirely possible without love.

Sam and Sally would be well looked after and if Grace didn't want to be involved then he would find a way to manage. But, despite his words, he wouldn't be involving Dan or Lucy.

The aroma of macaroni cheese wafted from the oven and Nick's stomach rebelled. Normally he enjoyed Grace's cooking, but he couldn't handle food in his present mood. He turned the oven off and grabbing some oven gloves he heaved the heavy dish on to a protective mat on the new kitchen bench.

Her deception made heavy inroads into his peace of mind. Even if Lucy was the best choice to look after the twins, Grace should have been up-front about her connection with Dan. They could have solved the transport problem without having Dan visiting on a daily basis.

He took a swipe at an innocent insect, which strayed on to the bench. No! There was only one reason for Grace to be secretive: she was attracted to Dan and knew that Nick disapproved.

He quashed any uncomfortable thoughts that he wasn't Grace's keeper and had no right to dictate how she lived her life. In a way he *was* her keeper in the monetary sense and he felt that she owed her loyalty to him and the babies.

How about all the unpaid work she did? A little demon

on his shoulder seemed determined to pinpoint the unreasonable aspects of his argument. The sparkling kitchen seemed to mock him and the golden crusty macaroni cheese virtually leered at him from the bench. He lurched off to his office remembering his Uncle Will's words that women and babies put a shaft through the stability of one's life.

The morning sun streamed in the bedroom window. It was a beautiful day making a mockery of Grace's depression. She had scarcely slept and her head ached almost as much as her heart. The baby gurgles and chatter emanating from the nursery brought her responsibilities to the forefront with a vengeance.

At least Sam and Sally were more civilised about their morning feed now, slotting into the routine that she had forged without any drama. Getting out of bed was the worst part, but once Grace began the day her spirits lifted. She managed to feed the twins without Nick's help and presumed he had slept in.

The macaroni cheese was adorning the kitchen bench and she suppressed a shudder. If Nick had eaten the previous evening there was no evidence of it. His absence was beginning to worry her. Perhaps he'd opted out. Common sense kicked in as she realised he was unlikely to move out of his own home. She was about to check his room when he emerged from the shed striding towards the house. His entire body language screamed hostility and his expression was grim.

'Pump works,' he said in a clipped tone, brushing past her.

As a morning greeting it left a lot to be desired, but at least it was a communication of some sort. He'd showered, dressed and left in thirty minutes and as Grace watched

Lucy trudging up the long drive from the front gate she thought Dan might as well have driven her to the door.

'He left early,' she told Lucy as she opened the front door.

'In a miff, I suppose,' Lucy said as she dumped her bag on one of the leather chairs. 'I suppose he's not even talking to you.'

'Oh yes. We had a scintillating conversation,' Grace told her. 'He said, "Pump works".'

Lucy burst out laughing. 'You're a real survivor, Grace. You'd need to be to live with Nick. He's anti just about everything you care about.'

A smile flitted across Grace's face. 'He's actually quite a caring person. Being landed with twins was a terrible shock to his system and his way of life, but he's accepted that.'

'He's lucky to have you to put in a good word for him,' Lucy said. 'The general consensus around here is that he's pretty ruthless.'

'But he's providing employment. Surely that's a mark in his favour?'

Lucy shrugged. 'Yes, I guess so, but I think he expects a high standard of output.'

'I can't see anything wrong with that as long as he's fair about it.' Grace thought of his harsh conversation with a female employee and his obvious annoyance when she provided Dan and Joe with cups of tea. Perhaps he was unreasonable and if that were the case he would make some enemies.

Lucy laughed. 'Do some of the lazybones around here good to do a full day's work. As my employer, I've got no complaints about Nick except for his aversion to my cousin. But, to be fair, Dan can be a bit overpowering.' She picked up the basket of dirty clothes and made her way to the laundry. 'Better keep up the standard,' she said, 'I'll get this lot into the machine.'

By the time Grace had cleaned up the bedrooms, settled the babies on a rug on the floor and made up some bottles, it was almost an hour later. Lucy's coffee addiction was almost as bad as Nick's, so Grace retrieved the coffee plunger and measured in some ground coffee beans, wondering if she dared use decaffeinated coffee. She shook her head. No! Lucy was more discerning than Nick and would detect the switch at once.

The water had just boiled when the back door was hurled open and Lucy raced into the kitchen.

'Fire!' she gasped. 'All the dead trees and dry grass are ablaze.'

Grace ran from the kitchen suddenly aware of the smell of smoke through the open door.

Once outside she fought against panic. It was much worse than she expected. Although the fire had started along the fence-line it was spreading rapidly through the dry grass.

Lucy ran to grab a garden hose, luckily still fixed to an outdoor tap, swiftly turning on the water and aiming it at the side of the house, hoping to prevent sparks from igniting its wooden frame. Grace briefly thought of the fire pump, but having no idea how to use it and no time to find out, suddenly recalled seeing some hessian bags in the garage. A moment or two later, she was yelling at Lucy to turn the hose on the bags, before frantically beating at the edges of the fire with the wet sacks.

'If it gets much closer, we'll have to abandon the house and get Sam and Sally out of here,' she cried. 'I'll take my car to the other side, so we can leave in a hurry.'

She glanced towards the house. Despite all the turmoil it had become her home. Moreover, she suspected that it was the first house which Nick had called 'home' in a long time. She brushed a grimy hand across her face. There was no time for sentimentality; the only thing that mattered was keeping Lucy and the twins safe.

The Rover suddenly appeared out of the smoke, and Grace wept with relief. Nick threw himself out of the vehicle and disappeared into the shed. The short length of time it took him to get the fire pump in operation by using the dam water, seemed almost miraculous to Grace, and when they finally had the blaze under control she leaned against the Rover and laughed.

'Warped sense of humour,' Lucy said. 'What's so funny?'

Grace waved a hand towards the fire pump. 'The "Pump works",' she said.

Lucy laughed too. 'We've got help,' she commented waving towards the fire truck, which had joined Nick in putting out the embers.

'I think it's the Bush Fire Brigade,' Grace said. 'Someone must have reported the fire.'

'Never mind who reported the fire,' Nick said later as he swallowed his cup of coffee. He paused as he drank, a puzzled look on his face. Grace held her breath. She had tried to avoid giving him the 'real McCoy', but Lucy had made the coffee and out-manoeuvred her.

Nick's attention swung back to the fire. 'What I want to know is who started it.'

'Surely it was spontaneous,' Grace said. The thought that the fire might have been accidentally, or worse, deliberately lit hadn't occurred to her.

'It's possible,' Nick said, 'but the fire brigade think otherwise.'

'You mean someone could have flung a cigarette butt down?' Lucy put her cup down. 'But, none of us smoke.'

'Exactly.' Nick ran an agitated hand through his hair. He hesitated before going on. 'You realise we could have lost the house?' He paused before adding, 'Not to mention the danger you were all placed in.'

Grace shivered. 'I was terrified the house would catch fire, but even more worried about Sally and Sam.'

'You should have all got in the car and left the property,' Nick said. 'The house is unimportant. It's also insured.'

'But, it's your home,' Grace said.

Nick looked around and shrugged. 'Houses are replaceable,' he said. 'People are not.' Eventually he went back outside and poked around among the embers.

'Not convinced it started spontaneously,' had been the Fire Chief's words, but he hadn't come up with any evidence to support his opinion. Nick worried away at the problem. A cigarette from a passing car wouldn't have been the cause because the fire had started well up the track near the house.

His decision to install the fire pump had been a lifesaver. Nick closed his eyes as a picture of what might have happened intruded into his mind. He opened his eyes and let them roam over the now blackened landscape. His fists clenched at his side. The risk would have been considerably less if he'd kept the grass down and installed a watering system.

Scenes and the emotions they'd triggered kept flitting through his mind. The anguish he'd felt when he saw Grace bravely battling the flames with wet bags. The sheer terror for her safety, and that of the babies and Lucy, as he'd pushed the Rover to its limits on the rough track.

He'd been in danger before. Almost lost his life in the shooting incident in the Middle East. Another few millimetres and the bullet would have been fatal. Somehow it was different when he controlled his own destiny.

Now he was responsible for others and the thought over-whelmed him. He'd been responsible for his brother. Haunting pictures of the last moments of his brother's life flashed into his mind.

The groan escaped his lips before he could cut it off. His technique for surviving the trauma of his past was slowly disintegrating. It was as if his body had been frozen for years: impervious to pain or deep seated feelings. The thaw had definitely begun the day Grace and the twins arrived on his doorstep and feelings of panic assailed him as he realised there was no going back.

It had been the result of soul searching that had caused him to return home unexpectedly. Nick shuddered as he realised the importance of a decision that had been little more than a whim at the time. Working had been impossible with his concentration shot to hell after his altercation with Grace.

Taking one last look at the mess caused by the fire Nick turned and went inside. Everything looked so normal it was almost an anticlimax.

'You OK?'

Grace was standing by the sink washing the coffee cups and she turned as he spoke and nodded.

'Why don't you put them in the dishwasher?' Nick said trying to control his irritation. 'I had it installed to save you work.'

She smiled. 'It only takes a minute to wash them and I like dabbling in the soapy water.'

'It'll give you dishpan hands,' Nick said.

After drying her hands on a tea towel Grace held them out. They were roughened from hard work.

Nick took her hands in his. 'Gracie, I came home early to apologise. I was out of line. I told you to employ a nanny and you chose the best. Whatever my feelings are towards

Dan they shouldn't involve you.'

'Dan is just a friend, Nick.'

He released her hands. 'It's none of my business.'

Her heart fell with a thud. He didn't care what her feelings towards Dan were. It was more a power thing with Nick. He needed to be in control and Dan with his easy going determination threatened that control.

'Just as well you did,' she said forcing her voice to sound bright. 'Lucy and I would never have coped.'

'You were doing a pretty good job when I arrived,' Nick said. 'I meant what I said. Don't ever put material possessions first. They mean nothing to me.'

A picture of him carefully placing Uncle Will's crystal bowl on the table flashed into her mind. It certainly had some powerful sentimental pull over him.

The slamming of the back door interrupted her thought pattern and they both turned as Lucy spoke.

'Good thing for the neighbours that the fire didn't jump the fence. The old adage about the grass being greener on the other side seems to be true.'

'That's because they have an automatic watering system near their house,' Nick said. 'Something I need to do as soon as possible. They keep their grass mown or slashed, another precaution where bush fire is concerned.'

'Maybe that guy I saw is keeping an eye on their property, even picking up their mail,' Lucy said.

Nick's head swung towards her. 'What guy?'

'The one I saw near the mail box next door,' Lucy said. 'Very dark complexion, downright unfriendly if you ask me.'

'That description doesn't fit any of the neighbours,' Nick said.

'No,' Grace took a deep breath. 'But, it fits the man Dan spoke to near our letterbox while we were having the extensions done. He was asking after someone, but Dan didn't like the look of him.'

'Dan should have mentioned it,' Nick said.

'He told me to,' Grace said quietly. 'I'm sorry. It didn't seem important at the time.'

Nick was silent for a while. 'It probably isn't important,' he said.

Grace bit back her surprise. Although she hadn't given Dan's warnings much credence the whole thing seemed to take on a different aspect the second time around. If it hadn't been for the disharmony caused by Dan's appearance yesterday she probably would have told Nick about the man Lucy had seen. That Nick didn't seem particularly interested in the man seemed out of context considering the fact that they had all been exposed to considerable danger because of a fire that could have been deliberately lit.

Perhaps his lack of interest stemmed from a knowledge of who the man was and that her theory that he was a private detective wasn't so ridiculous after all.

'As you suggested,' Nick said. 'He's probably keeping an eye on their property.'

He turned and left the room, resuming his poking around outside and Grace had an uneasy feeling that he hadn't wanted to extend the discussion on the man hanging about for some reason of his own.

Over the next few days Grace found it hard to settle. Normal everyday tasks seemed to be so much harder to cope with and small problems assumed mammoth proportions. At any time she expected Nick to deny parentage of the babies and hurl them all out on to the street.

Normally rational and sensible she tried to reason with herself. Why would he wait so long to make a decision about the twins' future allowing everyone to lapse into a false sense of security? His attitude towards the twins was caring and responsible. She was between a rock and a hard place. If she started questioning him he might start to have doubts about her faith in her sister's story.

Perhaps it was the aftermath of the fire, but everyone seemed edgy. Dan had no inhibitions about driving Lucy up to the door and he kept prowling around like some jungle cat on the loose.

'What's his problem?' Grace said as she and Lucy watched him walk past his truck and wander over to the burnt out area. 'He'll be late for work on the building site.'

'As he's always at great pains to point out,' Lucy said with a wry smile, 'it doesn't matter when you're in charge.'

'There's nothing very interesting about an area of burnt out trees and grass,' Grace said.

'Maybe he's trying to work out the best way to prevent it happening again.'

'Nick's already arranged for someone to come in and slash the paddocks and mow close to the house.'

'A bit like shutting the stable door after the horse has bolted,' Lucy said.

'He's had a lot on his plate,' Grace fired up. 'He can't do everything.'

'I know' Lucy said. 'He's probably used to thinking of himself as a single unit. At present his main interest in life is making a success of his business.'

She had that right, Grace thought. Fire prevention had probably been given top priority at the factory.

Dan eventually left, pulling up on the track to speak to the driver of a truck and trailer making its way towards the house.

'Now what?' Grace said, as the truck finally made it to the front door.

The large individual who emerged from the driver's seat looked more like a night-club bouncer than the mower man, but he had the tools of trade in his trailer and a set of directions in Nick's handwriting to prove his authenticity.

'Name's Bob Fisher,' he said. 'I'll be around for a few days.'

'The mowing will take a few days?' Lucy voiced the question Grace had been about to ask.

'There's landscaping and tree planting and a watering system to put in. More like a couple of weeks.'

Grace gave up and left him to it. She had no sooner gone inside than Nick rang. Yes, the mower man had arrived she told him, and yes – Dan had driven Lucy to work. She waited for the explosion, but it wasn't forthcoming, so she hoped Nick had accepted the situation. He sounded surprisingly docile, but if he'd had a change of heart she wasn't going to knock it.

He arrived home early clutching a box of fruit. 'I pass the stalls outside the plantations every day, so I decided to buy some.'

It was typical of Nick that he'd bought some of almost everything. Pineapples, strawberries, custard apples, bananas. Grace didn't mind. She enjoyed fruit and she intended introducing more of it into Sam and Sally's diet at the earliest opportunity.

Nick had the same idea. He stood at the sink mashing up some ripe bananas. 'They eat mashed up pears and apples,' he said. 'Bananas should be OK as long as they're ripe.' He frowned as if suddenly not sure of his new-found confidence where the babies were concerned. 'Shouldn't they?' he added

At seven months old, the twins were eating a variety of

food. So Grace couldn't see anything wrong with mashed banana. She usually checked with the clinic, but Sam and Sally had never reacted to any food. She nodded. 'Of course.'

'At this rate I'll need to start my own plantation,' Nick said as Sam gobbled up the new fare. Sally was more lady-like in her portions, but she enjoyed the banana too.

The whole episode left Grace with a warm glow. The interest Nick had shown in the twins' welfare wasn't that of a man hell bent on getting rid of them. She went to bed in a more settled frame of mind putting her previous attack of nervous tension down to the trauma of the fire.

For the first time in ages she fell into a deep sleep. As the ear splitting yells pierced her consciousness she sat up completely disorientated. Sally and Sam had been sleeping through for weeks now and she was totally unprepared for the violent interruption to her sleep.

'Grace!' Nick's bellow was barely below panic level and she hurled herself out of bed and charged into the nursery.

He was holding Sam who was screaming and throwing himself around. His little face was beetroot red and he was obviously in pain.

Grace took him and patted and soothed him, but nothing worked for long. When he threw himself backwards and then stiffened in a spasm of pain she almost panicked herself.

'Nick, I'm worried. I think we'd better find a doctor.'

He grabbed Sally who had joined her brother in chorus of sympathy and headed for the car.

'My car,' Grace said. 'I removed the baby seats from your car, and they're now in mine.'

Nick's description of her vehicle and its performance was less than complimentary as they raced towards the local hospital's emergency department. Once there, Nick swung into the car park and Grace breathed a sigh of relief that, because of the lateness of the hour, there were plenty of parking spaces close to the entrance. Not that a lack of space would have deterred him, she thought as he snatched Sam from his seat. He was perfectly capable of breaking every rule in the book when it suited him.

Keeping up with Nick as they strode through the glass doors of the hospital was a mission impossible as he demolished their red tape to ribbons and organised immediate medical attention. Grace caught up with him as he all but threw Sam into the doctor's arms.

'He's extremely ill,' Nick said. His deep voice held a tremor Grace had never heard before and under his tan he looked pale.

'It's important to remain calm,' the doctor said.

'You remain calm,' Nick yelled. 'It's not your child who's ill.'

Grace put a hand on his arm and she heard him draw in a deep breath. 'Sam needs you Nick.'

She almost gasped as he turned to her. Never had she seen such anguish on anyone's face. How could she have doubted the depth of his feelings for Sam or Sally?

'I'm almost sure it's a severe attack of colic,' the doctor said. 'When did you last feed him and what did he eat.'

'Bananas!' They both spoke at once.

'Were they ripe?' The doctor frowned and the anguish on Nick's face deepened.

'Yes,' Grace said. 'We thought it would be all right.' She looked at Sally who had gone back to sleep in her arms. 'Sally had banana too, but not as much.'

'Well this little chap has reacted rather badly,' the doctor said. 'I'd steer clear of banana where he's concerned. You'd better be cautious about new foods. He may have other intolerances.'

'I shouldn't have let him eat so much.' Nick spoke more to himself than anyone else and Grace knew he was blaming himself for Sam's attack of colic.

'I'd like to keep him here for an hour or so,' the doctor said. 'I'll give him some medication and see if that settles him down.'

They waited in a small room set aside for parents and Nick prowled like a caged animal until the doctor declared Sam well enough to go home.

Both the babies slept on the way home and Grace lay back in her seat and closed her eyes. Perhaps these dramas were par for the course with babies, but she would have to be more cautious with introducing new foods. A memory of Karen covered in hives caused by strawberries surfaced. Definitely a need to watch for allergies. Having sorted out in her mind how Sam's problem had arisen and how she would take steps to prevent a re-occurrence she slept.

'How can you sleep after such a traumatic experience?' Grace jumped as her passenger door was wrenched open and Nick stood leaning in and eyeballing her in an outraged fashion.

'But…' She gathered her composure and slid out of the car. 'Sam's fine now, Nick.'

'No thanks to me,' Nick said gathering him out of his car seat. He marched off leaving Grace to retrieve Sally.

Just what she needed? Nick had obviously decided to blame himself for something neither of them could have predicted. If anything she was to blame. She should have remembered that Karen couldn't eat certain foods although the difference in their ages had meant that she couldn't remember what Karen couldn't eat as a young child.

They put the twins to bed in silence and Grace was ready to fall into bed herself when she heard Nick filling the kettle in the kitchen. A glance at her watch revealed that it was three o'clock in the morning. It would seem he was determined to castigate himself and rob both of them of what little chance they had to sleep. With a sigh she made her way to the kitchen.

She straightened her shoulders before she entered the room. Ten minutes maximum. That's all it should take to sort him out and end the self-flogging he seemed hell bent on administering. No doubt he was a bit frayed around the edges from their unexpected ordeal, but she could soon fix that. It was only with hindsight that she realised she couldn't have been more mistaken.

chapter twelve

She stood in the doorway watching as he retrieved a mug from the nearby shelf. 'If that's tea, you're making I'll join you,' she said.

'It's coffee and before you tell me it'll keep me awake, I am aware of that. I'm not likely to sleep anyway.'

Not a good start. She wasn't about to enlighten him on the coffee either. Without caffeine it shouldn't keep him awake. 'Nick there's absolutely no point in worrying about what happened tonight. Sam's fine, and you weren't responsible for his problem.'

The noise of the mug hitting the table as he sat down startled her, but the pain on his face robbed her of breath. She sat close to him taking his hands in hers. 'Nick you've got this way out of proportion.' She repeated. 'You were not responsible for Sam's problem.'

'No, just for his death.'

Her head spun. What was he talking about? Sam was in his cot sleeping peacefully.

She gripped his hands hard. 'Sam's not dead, Nick.'

'Yes, he is. He's dead and it was my fault.'

His brother. He was talking about his brother. 'You didn't kill him, Nick.' She knew he could not have killed his brother. She didn't care what he was saying. She knew.

His eyes were looking at her, but she knew he was seeing back into the past. 'He was in the prime of life and I took him to Saudi Arabia and he died there.' The anguish on his face was heart rending and whatever had caused his brother's death Nick had yet to come to terms with it.

Grace pulled his hands against her breast, resting them there, her own hands folded over his. 'Tell me, Nick. Tell me what happened.'

He closed his eyes for a moment and then they opened. She had never seen such pain. It tore at her heart. How could she have thought him cold and ruthless?

'I had to take him with me Grace. He'd left the farm and moved to the city. He started running around with a fast crowd known for drug use and my father was at his wits' end. They had both been badly affected by the recent death of my mother.'

He paused and she wondered why he had left his own feelings out of the equation. Had his mother shown him so little love, that her death hadn't caused him to react in an adverse way? Or was it his strong character, which helped him to cope when others folded under the strain? She cut off the direction her thoughts were taking as he began to speak again.

'Sam had been the centre of her existence and he was like a ship without a rudder. I thought that if I found him a job on the project and kept an eye on him, he would get his act together.'

She felt the tension in his fingers and she ran her thumbs over them. He drew in a deep breath. 'I should have known better. We ran into trouble with the project, mostly due to terrorists who clearly had a vested interest in its failure. I think…I think that Sam may have accepted money to sabotage some of the work we were doing.'

'What!' Grace couldn't comprehend what he was saying. His own brother was capable of working against him? Possibly endangering Nick and his staff. 'Your brother would do that?'

Nick shrugged. 'I now realise that he must have had second thoughts, because he obviously didn't carry out whatever plan they'd settled on. So, I'm almost sure that his accident was a payback.'

Grace swallowed. 'He was killed in an accident?'

Nick's fingers gripped hers causing her to wince, but he didn't notice. 'A cable snapped and a heavy drum fell on him, killing him instantly. I don't believe it was an accident, but although I tried there was nothing I could do to prove it.'

He eased the pressure of his grip on her fingers and let out a long breath. 'I should never have taken him there. Working and living in a foreign country is never easy and often fraught with risk, and Sam was immature. Despite the fact that we had a reasonable relationship, he resented my success and the fact that Uncle Will left me all his money.'

There was silence for a while and she could hear the old kitchen clock ticking in the background.

'Your Uncle Will…?' she prompted.

He nodded. 'Will was my father's brother. He was an engineer and I followed in his footsteps.'

'Nick, it was clearly beyond your control. It wasn't your fault. You must accept that. You did what seemed to be the right thing at the time. I think you were very responsible.'

He shook his head. 'No! I made a bad decision, Grace – and it cost Sam his life. My father will never forgive me.'

His grip on her hands had loosened and Grace hoped and prayed that talking about his family tragedy had helped to ease some of the burden. He shouldn't have had to face the aftermath of this terrible trauma alone, but if he was alienated from his father where could he turn? Her thoughts turned momentarily to Karen, but she was convinced now that her relationship with Nick couldn't have had any depth even if it had resulted in twins.

'Nick don't you have any family you can turn to for support?'

He gave her a wry smile. 'No. Will was always my back-stop. He paid for me to go to boarding school and eventually to university. It was a foregone conclusion that I'd follow his example and become an engineer. In a way that only widened the division with my family. My father is the only one left and he has to pay for help on the family farm.'

'So you have no contact with your father.'

'Only when I send him…' He stopped mid-sentence. 'Only when I write to him.'

He sent his father money. Although he didn't complete the sentence Grace knew that was what he had almost said. He still cared about his father despite his lack of support. How could any parent having lost one son completely alienate the one they had left? And what about his Uncle Will? Had he helped or interfered?

'Your Uncle Will…' she paused uncertain what she wanted to ask.

'He's dead.'

'I realise that,' she said. 'The Waterford bowl. He left it to you didn't he?'

'He left me everything. He resented the fact that my father almost ignored my existence.'

What would have happened without his Uncle Will? No wonder he treasured the bowl. Grace nodded. 'If he'd been alive he would have supported you when Sam was killed.'

Nick smiled a twisted smile. 'He would have said to put it behind me. Life can be a bitch he used to say. Live for the moment. Make something of yourself. He laid down the ground rules and I followed them.'

'You can't live your life to someone else's blueprint,' Grace said. 'People are different. What makes one person happy doesn't work for others.'

'That seems to be the case with you and Karen,' Nick said. 'It's difficult to believe you were sisters.'

Gently she let his hands slide from hers as she stood up. She didn't want to discuss her life or her sister. Nick's shocking revelation was enough to cope with for one night. He looked dazed and exhausted.

She picked up his empty mug. 'I'll make that coffee.'

While she boiled the water and measured out the granules he remained in his chair. It was almost as if he didn't see her and she knew that he was still brooding about the past.

When she placed the steaming mug in front of him he looked up and the expression on his face tore at her heart. She had to find a way to help him.

Cautiously she took a sip of her own coffee. It was hot and it burnt her throat as she swallowed it. Her voice was husky when she spoke, but it seemed to draw his attention to what she was saying.

'Nick, that's why you held Sam at arm's length isn't it? You were afraid of getting too attached to him.'

Her perception brought forth a wry smile. 'Playing analyst now, Grace. I guess it doesn't take a psychology degree to work that one out.'

'But, you're so good with the twins, Nick. We'd never have managed without your help.'

He shook his head. 'Think about it, Grace. You narrowly escaped being bitten by a snake. I was the one who hadn't cut the grass.'

'And I was the one who took them into the danger in the first place,' she reminded him.

He went on determined to wear the hair shirt. 'I decided to take you to the beach and we were nearly the victims of a fatal accident.'

'Nick, it was an accident or the prank of irresponsible louts.' His eyes narrowed and she wondered what he was thinking.

'Then there was the bush fire. I should have had a fire prevention scheme in place weeks before.'

Grace almost swore. His brother might be dead, but the legacy of guilt he'd been left with was alive and well. 'You did install the fire pump and you came home in time to put the fire out.'

'All sheer coincidence and nothing to do with discharging my responsibilities. And then there was the bananas.'

'Oh, forget the bloody bananas,' Grace raged. 'It was only a matter of time until I shoved some down his throat so stop dredging around for reasons to flog yourself.'

They had both let their coffee get cold and Grace gathered up the mugs and went over to the sink. Nick came and stood behind her as she poured the dark liquid down the plughole.

His arms slid around her waist and he pulled her back against him. She felt his chin resting on the top of her head.

'Thanks for listening, Grace. It's the first time I've talked about losing Sam.'

She turned in his arms putting her hands on his shoulders. 'You need to talk about it, Nick. Unfortunately family tragedies happen all the time, but you can't bury them inside.'

'But I can make sure that I'm not the cause of any more.'

Her eyes widened at his statement. Even if he did accept that the twins belonged to him her gut feeling was that he intended to distance himself from them. She cursed Sam's unexpected food reaction. Nick didn't realise it, but he'd been getting more and more involved with the twins and he had unconsciously taken on much of the responsibility of their upbringing.

Grace was afraid that if she didn't do something he'd slowly withdraw from their lives. Oh, he'd provide financial support just as he did with his father, but he'd retreat into his protective shell so that he couldn't feel again the pain of guilt and what he perceived as failure.

Uncle Will hadn't helped either. He'd reinforced the dangers of permanent relationships and responsibility. Grace made up her mind. She'd give Uncle Will a run for his money.

She lifted her arms from his shoulders and slid them around his neck. He went to speak, but she wasn't listening to any more of the trash his relatives had brainwashed him with.

Standing on tiptoe she pressed her lips to his. His response almost wiped her out. She should have realised how vulnerable he was. Her blood was drumming in her ears, but she heard his agonised groan. She felt the pain of crushed lips and tongue as his mouth ravished hers. She clung to him offering no resistance as he hauled her against him, his hands kneading her buttocks and pulling her closer, closer. When his mouth left hers she drew in a harsh gasp of air only to feel breathless again as she felt his lips trail down her neck. His tongue lapped at the hollow below her throat and as he pulled her top open and kissed the curve of her breasts she knew she had pushed him too far.

Was she prepared to let him love her, possess her? It wouldn't be love because he'd been inoculated against love. She wanted desperately to give herself to him. To show him that he meant everything to her. Instinctively she knew that would be the last thing he wanted. Her hands slid into his dark thick hair holding his head against her breast and she moaned with the pain and the pleasure.

She felt him pause and look up and she licked her lips tasting the salt of blood. Nick noticed it too.

'God!' He thrust her away. 'Your lip's bleeding. I'm sorry.' He strode to the doorway shaking his head. 'I'm little better than an animal. Stay away from me, Grace.'

The door of his bedroom slammed. He'd locked himself away from any involvement with her – just as he shut himself off from any relationship which involved his deepest feelings.

Nick leaned against the bedroom door his heart hammering like a piston. He could still feel the brush of her lips when she kissed him. He slammed his fist into his hand. How could he have lost control like that? Damn! Had she no idea of the effect she had on him?

Pushing himself away from the door he went and lay on his bed. His head was throbbing from the trauma of the past few hours. Seeing Sam in pain like that had really shaken him. If it hadn't been for Grace's quiet calm he didn't think he would have coped.

He put his hands up to his head pressing his forehead almost if he could contain the thoughts that were screaming to be released. It was no use. He'd spent the past months suppressing the memories and he realised now that he should have worked his way through them and found some way of putting the trauma behind him. Telling Grace had helped, but he knew he had a long way to go. At no stage had she blamed him and that meant everything to him.

Perhaps he *could* put the past behind him, and end the hell which he'd lived with? It would take time and he needed to put some space between himself and Grace. Thoughts of her filled his mind and he cursed as his body responded. Her beauty was so much more than surface deep. She deserved better than him.

A picture of Dan, smiling, confidently handling the twins, flashed through his mind. Squeaky clean, wholesome, good living, Dan could claim all those attributes and probably more whereas he... He shuddered as his past came back to smack him in the teeth.

He'd lived life to the full, following Uncle Will's philosophy and look how it had ended up. A ready made family and the sweetest woman he had ever met, but right at the moment sharing his life with them on a permanent basis seemed as unattainable as the moon.

He sighed, a mournful sound that seemed wrenched from the depths of his soul. No, despite her caring, loving attitude towards him that night Grace would never want to join her life with his. He clenched his fists, but at least he could watch over her and keep her safe.

Grace slumped on to the kitchen chair. His reaction wasn't surprising now that she knew the truth about his background. What was surprising was how much he'd become involved up to that point. If it hadn't been for a series of minor setbacks he might have felt more confident about his role as a father.

For a moment she wished she had a couple of voodoo dolls. One of his mother who she suspected had shown him little love and one of Uncle Will. She'd stick so many pins in them they'd resemble pincushions. At least they were both dead.

Her breath whooshed into her lungs in horror at her thoughts. Was this the Grace that Karen had derided for her Christian outlook on life? For her desire to devote her life to the well being of others. When it came to the crunch Karen had known her better than she had known herself. Submission was something she couldn't handle and if Nick thought she was going to fade away into the background and let him retreat into his guilt ridden shell then he was in for a shock.

What ever it took she intended to help him back to normality. Uncle Will's memory might become a little tarnished in the process. She shrugged her shoulders.

Tough!

The twins had no conception of a bad night and lack of sleep. Grace groaned as she heard their early morning wake-up call. What had remained of the night she'd spent forming a battle plan to help Nick to cope with his traumatic past.

As she filled the twins' bottles she realised Nick had a battle plan of his own. He'd already left for work leaving a briefly worded note saying they were working flat out at the factory and he needed to be there early.

Hogwash! He was running away again. Was that why he had gone overseas to work? But he'd come back and he'd established a factory. That had a certain permanency to it and Grace realised with something of a shock that he'd done something out of character. Hope flooded her system and she began to hum as she fed the two babies.

Thoughts churned around in her head and her spirits rose as she realised that buying property and renovating it indicated a desire to throw down roots.

'Must be something in the water.' Lucy stuck her head around the door. 'Everyone's happy. Bob Fisher is out there planting trees and singing off key.'

Grace smiled. Happy was too strong an adjective, but she was hopeful and Nick had opened up to her. A plus in a long line of negatives.

'I wouldn't take too much at face value,' Grace said. 'We had a bitch of a night.'

Lucy looked surprised. 'You don't usually use strong words, Grace. Is Nick corrupting you?'

Grace smiled. 'You've been brainwashed by Dan. No, I guess realism is taking hold. I'm not the person I thought I was, but I don't intend to sink into depravity.'

'I'm glad to hear it,' Lucy said, taking hold of Sam and heaving him on her shoulder. 'Whew! He weighs a ton.'

As Lucy set about bathing the babies and doing their washing, Grace told her about their trip to the hospital.

'No wonder you look a bit wiped out,' Lucy said. 'Just as well I came early.'

Grace glanced at her watch. Lucy was at least an hour ahead of schedule.

'If it's OK with you, I'd like to leave early,' she explained. 'I want to buy a new outfit. I'm going out with this gorgeous hunk.'

'That's fine,' Grace said. 'Just as well it's pay day.' Lucy went to hang out the washing and Grace lifted down the Toby jug. She bit her lip. Damn! Nick had forgotten. There was no envelope with Lucy's money.

There was no way she was going to see Lucy miss out on her new outfit and Grace picked up the phone. She dialled the direct number that went straight through to Nick's office.

'Best speaking.' His deep clipped voice startled her causing her to draw in a sudden breath. She hated asking him for money.

'Grace, is that you?'

How had he known? 'Yes,' she said. 'I… Nick I need to pay Lucy and you forgot to leave her money.'

'Is that all?' She could hear the relief in his voice. 'I thought it was Sam again.'

'No, but Lucy's got a date and she needs her wages.'

'There's some money in my desk, Grace. The key is in my bedroom on the bedside table. I'll leave it to you to sort it out.' She heard the click as he put the phone down.

At least Lucy's problem was sorted out, but Grace felt a little fraught. Incidents like that made her realise how dependent she was on Nick and how tenuous her future was. She was in danger of seeing them as a family unit and she knew that just wasn't on. The last thing Nick wanted was to be part of a family circle and until she found some way of smashing down the barriers he had erected and drawing him closer he would remain on the outside.

Later in the day she went into his room to retrieve the key. For a moment she sat on his bed. It was enormous. He had finally bought the bed that he needed to accommodate his large frame and because the rooms in the old farmhouse were large it slotted into the refurbished room really well.

Thrusting aside thoughts of sharing the bed with Nick she searched for the key. There was a small photo on the table in an old fashioned frame. Grace held her breath. It was a photo of the twins. They were smiling, lying on cushions on the Persian rug.

She left the room and went into Nick's office thinking about the photo. Surely it was an indication of what the twins meant to him and that he accepted them as his children.

She inserted the key in the lock and opened the desk. It took a few minutes to find the money, but in the process of looking she realised that the photo meant nothing. Nothing at all.

chapter thirteen

The invoice lay face up, the private detective's name emblazoned on the top. It was simply an account for services rendered. There was no report, at least not attached to the invoice, but the breathtaking amount which Nick had paid indicated to Grace that he intended to leave no doubt who had fathered Sam and Sally.

She could almost taste the bitterness of her disappointment. He didn't trust her although she supposed his lack of trust was directed more at Karen. In some ways she couldn't blame him. Nothing about his past life had engendered trust.

For a moment she slumped into his office chair. Why the private detective? Why not a DNA test? It would have been much simpler and deadly accurate. She shrugged. Perhaps he didn't believe anything she had told him, but why had he been so caring and behaved in such a paternal way?

She thought again of the previous night and Nick's concern. Nothing added up and her head ached from trying to fathom things out. Wearily she boosted herself out of the chair and searched the desk for Lucy's money. She found a wad of notes in a small plastic bag and took what she needed, by-passing the invoice as if it were a loaded gun.

Lucy left early, her eyes sparkling with anticipation. Grace watched as she ran out to Dan, eager to get to the shops for an outfit to 'knock the hunk's socks off'.

Despite her depression Grace smiled. Her memory flitted back. She had never dated gorgeous hunks or tried life in the fast lane, but it had been her choice. She often wondered what track her life would have taken if Karen hadn't died and left her with the twins. She had always pictured herself as a teacher, but motherhood had not been a part of that picture.

The life she had carefully mapped out had been the pipe-dream of a teenager looking at the world through rose coloured glasses. It hadn't taken long for realism to rear its head. At least now she had no illusions about life and the role she would play. But the future was shrouded in uncertainty.

Asking Nick about the investigation didn't seem like a good idea. She wondered if he realised that she would have seen the invoice and worked out what was happening. She doubted it. He seemed pre-occupied with the factory.

Again she wondered why he didn't simply take a DNA test? She almost suggested it but balked at the last moment. Every minute she spent with him was precious and she wasn't doing anything to shorten her stay.

Days went by without any feedback on the investigation that she presumed was still taking place and Grace wrenched her belt in another notch. Common sense told her it was silly and irresponsible to let her problems affect her health.

It was a lovely day and the twins were having a nap. Lucy was singing in the kitchen as she prepared food for Sam and Sally. Grace smiled. Lucy, with her natural, happy disposition and cheerful outlook was in even more buoyant spirits since her date with the mystery man. Putting her head around the door Grace called out. 'I'm off to do some shopping. Can you cope for an hour or so?'

Lucy nodded. 'No problem. If I run into trouble I'll grab that hunk in from the garden.'

Grace frowned. She meant Bob Fisher. Her mind toyed

with Lucy's words. Hunk? She'd gone out with a hunk. Her breath hissed out. Had she gone out with Bob Fisher? He was certainly good to look at and extremely well built, but she doubted that he fitted Dan's rigid criteria. He was also a great deal older than Lucy. Suddenly little incidents that had meant nothing at the time took on a new significance. Lucy, exchanging light-hearted banter with Bob as she hung out the washing. Lucy, bent over some new addition to the landscaping, giving her opinion and Bob's serious expression as he took note of her suggestions. Yes! It was entirely possible that Bob and Lucy had something going between them, especially as Lucy was mature for her years and not attracted to the young men in her age group.

Her little car ran well considering how little use it got these days and Grace pulled into the car park at the local shopping centre. She loved the rural atmosphere and the friendly people. She paused to look in the window of the local coffee shop eyeing a piece of home-made carrot cake. Unconsciously her hand went to her flat stomach. Yes!

The table was inside near the huge glass window and as the waitress put the steaming cappuccino in front of her Grace leaned back in her chair and watched the people passing by. In all the time she had been living in the area she hadn't really met any of the locals so she didn't expect to recognise anyone.

She watched a young woman with two small children. They were about three and four years old. Not twins, but close in age. The woman held each child by the hand and guided them along, pausing to look in a pet shop window.

Grace picked up her cup easing her breath out in a huge sigh. It could be her in a few years time, but without help would she manage to keep her sister's children and what sort of life would they have with a substitute mother and no father? She forced herself to think one day at a time, silently vowing that nothing and no one would ever part her from Sally and Sam.

She sat forward and put the cup she had picked up back on the saucer. She recognised the truck minus its trailer that had stopped at a pedestrian crossing. Bob Fisher was behind the wheel and certainly not available as the back-stop Lucy had suggested.

Picking up her cup again Grace sipped her coffee. He'd probably needed to pick up some supplies for his work. She frowned as she realised what a permanent fixture he'd become. As soon as he finished one job Nick found another for him to tackle.

Once she'd finished her coffee and cake Grace went looking for clothes for the twins. They grew like weeds and whenever she could she spent her own money to provide them with what they needed. She felt even more reluctant to spend Nick's money when he doubted their parentage.

The shopping took longer than she anticipated and mindful of the fact that Lucy was on her own she hurried back to her car and unlocked it. She tossed her parcels on to the back seat and got in behind the wheel. The medical centre was across the road, an impressive building of bricks and glass that looked strangely out of place in the old fashioned town.

The sun's reflection off the glass caught her attention and as she gazed at the building the door opened and Nick came out. She sat completely still, the car key poised in her hand. Was he ill? Instinctively she knew that he hated going to the doctor.

It would have to be something of major importance to overcome that reluctance. Something like a DNA test? Her mind buzzed with questions. Wouldn't he have had to involve the twins? Wouldn't she have known? Slowly she

shook her head. If a man of Nick's intelligence and organ-
isational skills wanted to do something in secret, he'd find
a way.

She watched him stride up the street completely unaware
of her presence. He wouldn't have expected to see her
there. He knew she rarely left the twins.

Finally she inserted the key and the car spluttered into
life. It took all her concentration to drive home and in the
background her stomach churned and her spirits sank to an
all time low. As she drove up the driveway, now minus the
bumps, courtesy of Bob's efforts, she noticed his truck turn
into the property. If he'd driven home close behind her she
hadn't noticed, but then her whole mind was occupied with
the likely outcome of Nick's medical appointment.

Over the next few days in contrast to her own anxiety
and depression, Nick's spirits seemed buoyant. He was an
enigma. Didn't the outcome of the investigation and the
results of DNA testing mean anything at all? Or, maybe it
meant freedom?

As he handled the twins helping with their feeds and
playing with them on the floor, Grace found it difficult to
believe that he didn't want to keep them. There was a subtle
change in his attitude towards her. He was more relaxed.

There was a poignancy about the situation that tore at
her heart. How ironic if they became closer just before the
ties that bound them were severed. It made her wary. She
kept him at arm's length even though she sensed a slight
lowering of the barriers he had erected over the years.

She watched through the window as he stood talking to
Bob. Their sudden shout of laughter cut through her like a
knife. It seemed a lifetime since she'd felt like laughing
and she resented their ability to put life on the backburner
and enjoy the moment. They behaved as if they'd known

each other forever. She felt as if she were sitting in the middle of a large jigsaw puzzle and that half the pieces were missing.

Shrugging her shoulders she turned away. Her life might be in disarray, but she still had the responsibility of Sally and Sam and at the moment it felt like the world on her shoulders.

Nick saw her turn away from the window. He clapped Bob on the shoulder and walked towards the house. That she was desperately unhappy was obvious. But what was causing it? Mentally he'd listed all the possibilities and he had to admit there were a few starters among them. Perhaps laying all that grief on her shoulders had been too much, but it had opened the floodgates for him.

He'd had a few sessions with the counsellor now, and it had been unbelievable how it helped to lift the burden. He wanted to share his experience with Grace, but she was holding him at arm's length.

A wry smile twisted his mouth. Probably just as well considering the effect she had on him. It was more than physical. He realised now that his feelings were becoming involved as they never had before and for once he wasn't running scared. He needed to tread warily though especially as there were a few problems to sort out.

The smell of tea cooking attracted his attention as he opened the back door. He went into the kitchen where Grace was stirring something on the stove. The twins were sitting in their high chairs and Sally was sucking her fist and pausing periodically to omit a series of piercing yells.

He lifted Sally from her chair and put her up over his shoulder.

'Thanks,' Grace said. 'There's nothing more harrowing than trying to prepare a meal with one or both of them crying.'

She turned back to the stove. In her jeans and checked shirt she looked as neat and slim as always. Slim! Guilt swamped his system. She was still downright thin. Just lately he had thought that maybe she had put on a little weight giving her figure a slightly more curvaceous look, but now she looked just as she had when she'd first come to stay with him. At the end of her endurance. Why?

He felt that something was bothering her and unless she confided in him he could only guess at what it was. God knows there'd been enough weird incidents to affect anyone's sense of security. Surely having Bob around made her feel more protected. He sought for a way to get her to confide her worries.

'You must be exhausted,' he said. 'If the twins are unsettled we can always get a takeaway.' He grinned at her disgusted look. 'Everyone has takeaway in an emergency situation.'

'I don't think teething is an emergency, Nick.'

He peered into Sally's crumpled face. 'Is that the problem?'

'It's Sally's problem and I'm sure Sam will want to get in on the act, so I can expect some broken sleep.'

'I'll share with you,' he said. 'You can't do it all alone.'

Nick frowned. He couldn't believe it was worry about the twins' teething problems that had caused her obvious unhappiness and weight loss. Surely she knew that he wouldn't expect her to cope on her own.

A shiver passed over her slim frame. Doing it alone. The thought terrified her. Teething she could cope with, but a whole future on her own was unthinkable.

As if he had read her thoughts Nick turned towards the high chair and slid Sally back into it. 'She's stopped crying now. What can I do to help?'

Grace heaved a sigh of relief. 'If you could feed them I'll get on with tea. Their food is in a container on the table. It's the right temperature and I just use the one bowl and spoon.'

Nick picked up the bowl and peered at the bright orange contents. He gave Grace a questioning look.

'It's just mashed pumpkin and potato with some butter added. They had meat at lunchtime and they seem to like their vegetables. After that they can have custard and fruit.'

Nick nodded and carefully placed a bib around the neck of each twin amused when Sam's mouth opened expectantly. He shovelled in a spoonful of the food and it disappeared. Sally began to look indignant and he hastily spooned some food into her mouth. From then on it became rather mechanical with the spoon being plied from dish to open mouth in quite a rhythm. 'Nothing to it,' Nick said wondering why people made such a drama out of mealtimes with children. He shovelled another spoonful into Sam's waiting mouth frowning as Sam sat still and didn't swallow. He leaned closer looking into Sam's face. 'What…' he began. For a small child it was a Herculean sneeze and took Nick totally unawares. The orange paste hit him between the eyes and he looked at Grace in astonishment.

To say that it made her day was going a bit far, but she couldn't suppress the laughter as she grabbed a washer, dunked it under the tap and set to work to clean a face that was more often decorated with a five o'clock shadow than pureed pumpkin and potato.

'I should be paid danger money,' Nick grumbled. He took the washer and finished cleaning his face. There was danger all right, but it wasn't from a dirty face. Having Grace gently clean his face triggered all kinds of emotions and he decided it was time to make a quick exit.

'I can feed them their dessert,' she said sensing his discomfort.

As he left the room she wondered if it was being showered with food that had caused his mood change or whether coming to grips with the downside of parenthood was proving a bit much. She shook her head. What difference did it make? Her life at the moment seemed to be a succession of problems without any promise of resolution.

Somehow she got through the evening meal. Nick helped her put the twins to bed and he was so gentle and caring with them she wondered briefly if she was losing her senses. How could he be such a father figure if he was still denying parentage?

Desperate for sleep she became exasperated when her thoughts churned from one problem to another. Finally she fell into a troubled doze only to be woken by a wail that would have done a banshee proud. Barely awake she staggered into the nursery to find Nick by Sam's cot lifting him out.

She gave him a rueful smile. 'I told you he wouldn't let Sally hold centre stage. I'll get some teething jelly.'

Nick held him while she rubbed his gums and then he patted him to sleep. Grace leaned back against the door waiting to make sure that he didn't need help.

He looked up and smiled at her. 'Go to bed, Gracie. You look all in.'

Her heart did a series of loop the loops. His chin was shadowed with the beginnings of a dark beard, his hair rumpled, and he was barely covered with an old bathrobe. He looked drop dead gorgeous and she could have swallowed him in one gulp. She turned quickly and fled to the kitchen.

Filling the kettle with water, she tried to get herself under control. He was way out of her league. Despite the fact that she loved him with all her heart she wasn't oblivious to the difference in their make up and their values. She drew in a deep shuddering breath. Her own dreams and aspirations had come to nothing and her failure had left scars, but the principles that had led her down that path were still rock solid.

She took a mug and put a herbal tea bag in it. Hopefully it would help her to sleep. The kettle was boiling and she began to pour the water into the mug.

'Hey! I thought I told you to go to bed.'

Startled by Nick's sudden appearance her hand jerked and she poured the water over her other hand as it held the string on the tea bag.

To Grace it was the last straw. An agonised moan escaped her lips as she put the kettle down and clutched her hand against her chest.

Nick was beside her in seconds taking her hand and running it under the cold water. 'Just hold it there for a moment, Grace.' He disappeared, but was back in seconds with the first aid kit.

When he was satisfied that the cold water had eased her pain he applied some gel, gently covering the reddened area.

'I'm a thundering great idiot, love,' he said. 'Giving you a fright like that.'

Perhaps it was the 'love' or maybe just the touch of his hands, but Grace crumpled. She put her head against his chest and sobbed.

It seemed a lifetime that he held her, soothing, stroking and to Grace it felt like loving, but as normality returned she realised she was ready to read anything into what was simply comforting.

When the comforting changed to something more mean-ingful she wasn't aware, but she was certainly aware of the wild beat of his heart, and the evidence of his masculinity as she pressed against him. She raised her eyes, mesmerised by the dark desire, the longing in his. Whatever reservations she had, she felt as if she belonged in his arms.

There was no way she could hide the message her own eyes conveyed and she didn't want to. When Nick swung her up into his arms she offered no protest. Her head rested against his shoulder and she closed her eyes.

She knew before she opened them that he had carried her to his bedroom, and when she did open them she saw the question in his. Her smile was all the reassurance he needed and he placed her gently in the middle of his bed.

The deceptive tenderness of his kisses acted like a powerful aphrodisiac. She couldn't get close enough to him. Almost as if their two bodies could merge into a whole. He eased the straps of her night-dress down, his fingers brushing over the heavy gold cross and chain which she wore around her neck and she heard him gasp as her creamy breasts spilled out. His large tanned fingers gently caressed them, sending currents of unbelievable pleasure surging through her body.

She felt as if she had reached the pinnacle of love and happiness, but when she felt the warmth of his tongue moving erotically over her nipples, the threshold of her pleasure rose steeply.

'Oh Nick…!' she bit back the words of love she almost uttered. He wouldn't want to hear them. It wasn't love with Nick. She tensed slightly as uneasiness feathered through her system. It didn't matter that for him it was only a physical pleasure.

As if to reassure her, he stretched out a hand and stroked her cheek. The towelling sleeve of his robe caught on the gold cross. He tugged at it and the chain broke.

She sat up as the chain and the cross fell from her neck.

Catching it in her hand she stared down at it mesmerised.

'I'm sorry, Grace,' he said. 'Here, I'll put it on the bedside table.'

'No!'

She looked up at him with stricken eyes, and they both knew that her refusal meant more than the location of her chain. She slid from the bed, pulling the straps of her night-dress up over her shoulder.

'I'm sorry,' she whispered as she fled from the room.

He levered himself up intending to follow her, but every instinct warned him to leave her alone. He cursed himself for a fool. She'd been emotionally fragile for some time and although he'd genuinely wanted to help and comfort her, once he'd had her in his arms his own emotions had run out of control.

He sat heavily on the side of his bed. His body ached from his need of her. What was it about her that made him throw out all reason and self-discipline? He'd had women in his life before. Quite a few women, but not one affected him the way Grace did. When his association with them ended he'd walked away.

A shudder passed over his frame. Without a doubt he knew that he could never walk away from Grace. That in itself should have scared the hell out of him, but he realised it didn't. He swung his feet up on to the bed and lay back against the crumpled pillows. His thoughts churned relent-lessly. It was his own fault she'd become spooked.

Fool! He castigated himself. The reason she figured so largely in his life was because she was different. He needed to treat her differently. The thought that some of her recent anxiety might be connected with him did nothing for his confidence. Maybe it was fear of him coming on to her like some randy teenager that was upsetting her.

That thought was enough to put an end to any likelihood

of sleep although he couldn't quite equate her initial reaction to his lovemaking with revulsion. Mentally he examined every detail of the brief time they had spent in each other's arms. A big mistake, he acknowledged, as his body responded with a vengeance and he staggered from bed to bathroom to stand under a cold shower.

Grace opened eyes heavy from lack of sleep and glanced at her bedside table. The gold chain and cross glistened in the sunlight. Unconsciously her hand went to her bare neck. She always wore the chain. It reminded her of the good and the bad aspects of the battle she had lost. Last night it had reminded her of her ideals and values. More than anything she had wanted to give herself to Nick, but at the last minute she had balked. Her gift wouldn't have been received in the spirit with which it was given.

How was she going to face him? Everything was heading towards a climax where she feared she and the twins were going to have to leave and start all over again to forge some kind of life of their own. The sigh that escaped her was wrenched from depths. Did everything she set out to do have to end in failure?

She could hear him in the kitchen, but she couldn't avoid him forever and she needed to go there to prepare food for Sally and Sam. She just caught the muttered morning greeting as he left the kitchen, passing her in the doorway. She heard him hesitate in the lounge room and she peeped around the door. The sun was shining on the crystal bowl and guiltily Grace noticed the dust that had accumulated on its multi-faceted surface.

Nick must have noticed it too and he picked it up and carried it into the kitchen. Grace hid a smile. His housekeeping skills were almost non-existent, but that bowl was special.

He filled the sink with hot soapy water and washed the bowl. Grace was glad he was doing it. It would be just her luck to knock it and chip it. As she worked beside him in the kitchen she thought about the previous evening. No doubt he thought her a tease and it wasn't like that. She gulped in a deep breath. Perhaps she should try to explain. She owed him that.

The bowl was clean and sparkling and Nick lifted it from the bench. As he turned to leave the kitchen Grace spoke suddenly. 'Nick.'

He turned back and the words poured out. 'Nick. About last night. I'm sorry.'

An ironic smile passed over his face. 'It's all right, Grace. I was out of line.' He hesitated and then spoke again. 'Grace, I realise you're not into casual relationships. That you haven't had much experience with men.'

She drew in a relieved breath. 'No. I've had no experience with men, Nick, but it goes deeper than that. It's tied up with my past.'

He looked stricken and she realised he could be misinterpreting her words. 'Oh, it's nothing bad, but the whole experience was upsetting for me.'

He continued to look worried and she hastened to explain. 'When I began my noviciate I was so sure I would cope. That despite the fact that very few woman become nuns today…'

The bowl hit the floor and crashed into tiny pieces. Grace let out an agonised squeal.

'Oh Nick! Your beautiful bowl. I'm so sorry.'

He sagged against the kitchen bench totally oblivious to the fate of the bowl. One thought and one thought alone raged through his numbed brain. Last night he had come within a hair's breadth of making love to a nun.

chapter fourteen

The shock finally subsided and he straightened, clearing his throat. 'You should have told me,' he said. It explained so much. Damn her! She should have told him at the beginning. If it hadn't been for Karen… 'Did you leave to take over the care of the twins?'

She shook her head. 'I left about the time Karen needed me, but neither she nor the twins were my reason for leaving.'

He studied the expression in her wide green eyes. Was she telling the truth? She would have made the sacrifice, given up what to her would have been a vocation. Perhaps even now she had plans to go back one day. His mind threw up a series of incidents all significant now with the benefit of hindsight. She'd mentioned a father. Obviously a priest – not *her* father. She always wore the cross, probably the only link to her past. She'd had little money and had been forced to stay with friends.

'The friends you lived with after Karen died?'

'Sisters from the order which I had planned to enter. Most of them live outside the church in the community nowadays. And dress much more informally. It is different now, Nick, but even so I knew that I had made a mistake.'

'Are you sure about that?' He held his breath. He didn't want her to be a nun, no matter how altruistic her motives.

She nodded. 'Totally sure. I couldn't submerge my own personality in the demands of a religious calling. Despite what may seem like a gentle exterior, I can be stubborn about issues that are important to me. I couldn't agree with all their teachings. I'm not naturally submissive. There were a multitude of problems and I couldn't come to terms with them.'

He thought of the few times she'd stood up to him. Her quiet determination. Hell! He ate good food now, and drank decaffeinated coffee, although he wasn't letting her know he'd figured out her deception. He'd embraced fatherhood and was trying to work out how to involve Grace in a relationship.

His insides churned as he reassessed the likelihood of that happening. Now the terms of that relationship would be a whole new ball game. He'd realised that a relationship with Grace would be different, but she would want total commitment. The word 'marriage' became predominant in his brain and he shied at the thought. Uncle Will's dire warnings came rushing back. Uncle Will! Nick looked at the mess at his feet.

Grace followed his gaze. 'I feel really awful about the bowl, Nick.'

'It wasn't your fault,' he said. 'I was the one who dropped it.'

And I was the one who dropped the bombshell, Grace thought. She could imagine how living with an ex-nun would appeal to Nick. Her spirits hit an all time low as she thought she had just given him another reason for wanting to see the back of her. She turned away to retrieve the broom, but Nick was there before her.

'I'll do it,' he said. 'At least I won't have to clean the damn thing anymore.'

What could she say? The last thing Nicholas Best would do would be to let his feelings show, but she knew how important his Uncle Will had been to him and the bowl had been the only tangible reminder that Nick had kept.

The stubborn streak that she'd declared to Nick came

into play in the next few days. Whatever happened she would find a way to provide for the twins. She hadn't told Nick that she had invested more than herself in her short training as a novice. She had given her small inheritance to the poor, feeling that she should totally commit herself to the life she had chosen.

Nick strode around his property noting the changes to the landscape. Bob Fisher had done wonders especially as he was working outside his chosen field. He sat on a tree stump and tried to make some sense of his seething thoughts.

From the beginning he'd been painfully aware of the differences between his lifestyle and Grace's. That difference seemed to apply to every facet of his existence. There was the physical difference for a start. She looked so delicate, although he knew from personal experience that her fragility hid an iron clad will.

He leaned his elbows on his knees and rested his chin on his hands. The list was endless. They viewed life from a different perspective. Grace still believed in and trusted people. Although she had once said she didn't trust him she had trusted him when he could have taken advantage of her. But, he hadn't. He thought of the couple of near misses they'd had, but realised that he would never have forced the issue. Perhaps he wasn't a total loss.

She had a strong sense of family despite a less than perfect childhood and a sister who had been totally opposite in every way. His own childhood had been lacking in love although Uncle Will had stepped into the void. His family life had been totally fractured when Sam had been killed and there was nothing he could do to meld the family together again.

Nick's thoughts turned to Uncle Will, dredging around

in his mind for memories of the man who had directed his life. A big man in every sense of the word, he'd oozed confidence. An ability to meet the world head on. He had never appeared inadequate in any area of his life.

Instinctively Nick realised that appearances could be deceptive and that his uncle's desire to remain unattached could have stemmed from a traumatic earlier experience. Perhaps his only attempt at a relationship had failed and he protected himself by living on the fringe.

Nick stood up. That was what he was doing. His uncle had died a lonely man, with a wealth of material possessions and only one person in the world who really cared about him. Suppressing a shudder, Nick vowed that he wouldn't go down that road. Changing principles that had been ingrained for most of his adult life wouldn't be easy – but nothing worth having was likely to be easily obtained.

Grace stood at the window watching as Nick sat on the stump. It was clear that he was in the throes of some 'deep and meaningful' thoughts. Her confession had certainly thrown him and she suppressed a grin as she remembered the shattered look on his face. She had once likened him to the devil, but he still had his own code of ethics and it didn't involve sex with someone who had come within a hair's breadth of a life of chastity.

The smile faded as she thought of what had transpired between them. Sex. That's all it would have been for Nick. Although, for her...for her it would have been a natural culmination of the deep love which she felt for him.

As Nick stood up, she tensed. He would be coming inside and even being in the same room with him was like entering a torture chamber. She sighed with relief as she noticed Bob Fisher's vehicle coming up the track. Nick waited to speak to him and Grace turned away. They always seemed to talk together for ages, almost as if they had known each other for years.

Nick stood by the tree stump waiting for Bob to pull up beside him. He bent down and looked through the window. 'Got a minute?'

Bob unfolded his bulky frame from the car. 'Sure. Got a problem?'

Nick gave him a rueful smile. 'You could say that.'

Grace heard the back door slam as Nick came inside, realising with a sense of shock that an hour had passed since Bob Fisher had pulled up beside him. Surely they hadn't been talking all that time? What did they have to talk about? Their lifestyles would be poles apart. Shrugging her shoulders she finished folding the clean washing and went to look for Nick.

He was standing by the table where the crystal bowl had sat and, once again, feelings of guilt surged through her. Obviously, losing the bowl was hurting him and she wished she could do something to compensate. But how could she? There was nothing that could replace what had been almost a monument to his uncle.

'I think it was a good thing,' he said nodding his head at the empty space.

If he'd said that falling under a bus was beneficial, she couldn't have been more surprised. 'But, surely it was a special reminder of someone whom you loved?'

He gave her a lopsided smile. 'Loving someone shouldn't make you oblivious to their faults. Will had set ideas and he expounded at length about them until I absorbed his set of values. I realise now that his views could have been coloured by past experiences.'

Grace frowned. She wasn't sure where the conversation was heading.

He ran a hand through his hair. 'I'm a big boy now, Grace. It's time I made a few decisions of my own, unimpeded by Will's philosophies. It might sound silly to you, but I see the shattering of the bowl as somehow symbolic.'

It all sounded a bit deep to Grace, but she got the gist of what he meant. 'You mean the influence Uncle Will had on your life ended with the demise of his bowl…?'

'Something like that,' Nick said. 'More that one of the links to my past has been severed and I'm looking at a new start with a fresh outlook.'

Initially Grace just felt relief that he had handled the loss of the bowl so easily. It was only later that she really thought about what he had said. He'd talked about fresh starts. That could mean without any encumbrances. Which would be more Uncle Will's style though, and he'd indicated that any decisions he made would now be his own.

Her thoughts were still in a state of chaos when Nick's mobile phone rang, and soon afterwards he left in the Rover saying that he had an urgent matter to deal with.

Grace watched as he drove down the track, waving to Bob Fisher who was unloading his trailer and preparing to mow the grass. She sank on to the sofa wondering what crisis had evolved at the factory. They worked in shifts and Nick was always on call in an emergency, particularly on a weekend, but several things puzzled her.

Why spend so much time earlier talking to Bob Fisher, when he just came to take care of the grounds? As far as she knew, there was no big project for Bob to undertake at the moment. At least nothing which involved lengthy consultation. And why was Bob working at the weekends? It wasn't as if any of the landscaping – or, even in this instance, the mowing – was urgent. And yet, during the week Bob seemed to be there from daylight until dark. If Lucy had been around, she could maybe have suspected that he just wanted to be in close proximity to her. But Lucy didn't work at the weekends.

As Nick drove around the winding mountain road to his factory, his mind was concentrated on both his own future and the recent revelations about Grace's past. Would it be possible for them to make some kind of life together? He sighed. Their lifestyles and personalities couldn't have been further apart, not even if they'd come from two different planets. He bit down on his bottom lip.

OK, so he could make some changes, but his persona was deeply ingrained and even with the best will in the world, he knew that many of his characteristics were there for life. He also knew that there were some things he didn't want to change. What had made him successful for instance. Helped him go out and take life by the throat. His lips twisted in a smile. He may have lost his innocence early in life – but Grace clearly had enough for both of them.

His thoughts turned to the conversation which he'd had with Bob. His brow creased in a frown. Bob had really torn strips off him for not being up front with Grace about the twins. To leave her in limbo about their true parentage was, in Bob's opinion, nothing short of criminal. Nick realised that he was right. Since the day he had held Sam's little hand, he had known without a doubt that they were his brother's children.

The family curse, Sam used to call it. He was referring to his little fingers, which curved towards the adjoining finger rather than standing straight up. Nick's hands tightened on the steering wheel. His father's fingers had been the same. A genetic fault. Harmless enough, but apparently hereditary. Nick glanced down at his own little fingers. Straight as a die. For some reason he had managed to bypass that particular family gene.

Nick sighed. At first he had pushed the knowledge away, knowing that he could never turn his back on his brother's children. But, he'd been terrified of the commitment and the lifetime responsibility involved in looking after them. It was coming to terms with those issues, and the uncertainty of what part Grace would play in their future, which had kept him from taking her into his confidence. But, memories were continually rising to the surface of his mind. So much so, that he could no longer remain in a state of denial.

Those memories flashed into his mind as he drove. The old piano covered in baby pictures of Sam. The fact that Sam had looked exactly like his son. Nick fought to keep the bitterness from pervading his mind, but he wasn't having much success. There had been no baby pictures of him, the eldest son, on that piano – or anywhere else for that matter. He wondered again, as he had throughout his whole life, why he had been so unloved? However, when a possible reason presented itself, as always he quickly banished the thought.

The road curved sharply and he dismissed his turbulent thoughts to concentrate on his driving. The shoulders of the road were badly eroded from the recent rain, which meant that his large car took up more than its fair share of room.

A loud crack exploded through the air, sending a cloud of screeching parrots from their resting place in the trees, while at the same time he began to lose control of the car; his wheels skimming the unstable edge. Nick fought the bucking vehicle as he would have a wild beast, and victory was only partial as while maintaining its hold on the road, he sideswiped a large tree.

Stunned, he sat slumped over the steering wheel, a trickle of blood oozing from the cut on his forehead.

Despite his dazed mind, a strong premonition that danger was still lurking in the nearby hinterland, helped him to gather enough strength and force his head upright.

Sounds of crackling in the bushland rising above the road brought his muddled thoughts back on track, and he grasped hold of the door handle on the driver's side. It was the passenger side of the car which had sustained all the damage, and he was fairly certain the engine would be out of action.

As he rolled out on to the road, he heard a car pull up behind him. As a large man exited the car and came running towards him, Nick staggered to his feet and raised his arms, his hands forming fists.

'Whoa!' The man backed off as a plump young woman and a young child emerged from the car.

Nick's arms flopped to his side. He didn't think a potential killer would come accompanied by his wife and child. He stepped back and leaned on his car, his head was swimming and the pain around his rib cage suddenly manifested itself, robbing him of breath.

The man approached cautiously and his wife called out. 'I'm a nurse. We won't harm you.' She turned to her husband. 'He's obviously sustained a blow to the head. He's disorientated.'

No, Nick thought. He was thinking clearly, despite the blow to the head – and one clear thought came through in neon lights. Someone had just tried to kill him! He glanced again towards the surrounding bushland, but it was still and quiet. If someone had been lurking there, he felt sure that they would no longer be a threat.

Killing someone because of a past grievance was one thing, but killing an innocent family would be going too far. Especially as the publicity the situation was likely to generate, would obviously defeat the purpose of a crime intended to be disguised as an accident.

'How did it happen?' His large male rescuer seemed more interested in the rudiments of the mishap than Nick's physical condition, which he left to his wife to assess.

'Tyre blew out,' Nick mumbled. 'I almost went over the edge.' He gave the other man a rueful grin. 'I'm sorry if I over reacted. It must have been the knock on my head.'

'No worries.' A large paw was extended. 'Ned Williams. My wife's name is Jill and the young fellow here is Johnny.'

Ned walked slowly around the vehicle, concentrating more on the damage to the engine and bodywork and giving the blown-out tyre only a cursory glance. 'They really go when they blow-out, don't they. You'd think it'd been shot full of holes.'

Nick nodded. He didn't think the statement, that it had indeed been shot full of holes, would be likely to engender good relations and he needed their help.

Jill finished looking at the obvious injury to his head and went back to their car for a first aid kit.

'We'll take you to the hospital,' Ned said.

Nick shook his head. 'I'm OK.'

'No.' Jill appeared with plaster to apply to his head. 'You will have concussion and you also appear to have some rib damage.'

Nick looked at her in shock.

'I'm trained to pick up these things,' she told him firmly. 'You're having difficulty breathing and you're obviously in pain. It definitely means a visit to the hospital.'

Nick nodded. 'OK. I'll just make a call on my mobile phone. Let my…' He paused for a moment. 'Let my family know what's happened.'

Nick slid into the seat of his vehicle and rang Bob Fisher. He held the phone a distance from his ear, while that individual expressed his opinion of the turn of events.

Nick forbade him to leave Grace and the babies. As far as his Range Rover was concerned, it would have to take its chances – although he agreed to let Bob arrange for someone to come and tow it away.

Grace was slumped in the leather chair when Bob Fisher appeared at the door.

'Grace, Nick just rang me on the mobile. He's had a bit of an accident on the range road. He's OK,' Bob added quickly as he watched the colour leave her face.

'Is he hurt?' The words were a mere whisper.

'Only a bang on the head. And we all know how hard Nick's head is.'

It was only later that Grace realised the familiarity behind Bob's words. Scarcely the words of an employee about their boss.

'Where…?' Grace began.

'Nick's at the hospital, being checked out. Some people picked him up on the road. I'll arrange for someone to collect his vehicle, but it sounds like a tow job.'

Grace drew in a sharp breath. She felt sure that Bob was varnishing over the true facts. She was desperately worried about Nick. She wanted to go to the hospital. To be with him. But the twins were asleep and Bob was busy arranging for Nick's car to be towed away. She thought fleetingly of asking Bob to baby-sit. However, despite his many outdoor skills, where babies were concerned she doubted that he was likely to know which end was up.

She looked up at him, suddenly feeling that he was more than just the gardener. She blinked back her tears.

'Bob, he'll be all right, won't he? I can't leave the babies to go to the hospital.'

He threw a heavy arm across her shoulders. 'Of course

he'll be all right. He's survived worse than this and he wouldn't want you to leave the twins. They may be Sam's children, Grace, but Nick does feel just the same as if they're his.' He gave her arm a squeeze, saying as he left. 'I'd better get his car organised. It'll take some recovering from that area.'

Grace drew in a deep breath, collapsing into a nearby chair. Sam's children. The twins belonged to his brother! The words slammed around in her brain, causing her head to ache – but it was the ache in her heart that ripped her apart. He *knew* that the babies were not his. And yet, while he'd told their handyman-gardener, he hadn't told her.

It was now obvious that Nick had known Bob for a long time, and that they had a close friendship. But, to confide such a personal matter to him and not to tell her, the person who cared for and loved the twins with all her heart, left her feeling totally shattered.

Two hours later Nick arrived home. A taxi dropped him at the door and, despite her anguish, Grace rushed out – concern for his well-being overriding the turmoil she was feeling. She clasped his arm, recoiling when she heard his gasp of pain.

'What? Where?'

Gingerly he put an arm about her. 'Just a clout on the head and a couple of broken ribs. Nothing to get excited about.'

'Nick, what happened? It was an accident, wasn't it?'

He cursed her astuteness, but there was no way he could let her know the real facts.

'Of course. Why would you think otherwise? I just lost control on a crumbling edge. Maybe some recent rain has played havoc with the road.'

He explained about Ned and Jill Williams and how they

had come to his rescue.

'How fortunate that they came along,' Grace said. 'Goodness knows what would have happened if they hadn't.'

Nick suppressed a shudder. Amen to that. His attention was distracted as Bob Fisher arrived to tell him that his vehicle was being transported to a repair shop.

'Any problems?' Nick asked.

'No, not unless you count the loss of the vehicle's wheels. You can't beat these opportunist car thieves. They couldn't have had long to remove them.'

Grace was shocked. 'You're saying some thief took the wheels off the Rover, while it was waiting to be towed...?'

Bob nodded. 'Frankly Grace, I think the car will be a write off. Just be thankful that Nick didn't end up over the side of the mountain.'

Nick put a hand on Bob's shoulder. 'Thanks for your help. You'd better get off home now. I'll see you out.'

'You should rest,' Grace said moving towards the door.

'Gracie, do something for me, love,' Nick turned towards her with a lopsided grin. 'Make me a cup of tea, will you? My throat's dry as a desert.' He guided Bob to the door, relieved when she turned back towards the kitchen.

Once they reached outdoors, Nick said. 'He took the wheels off, huh.'

Bob nodded. 'So would you – if you'd shot the tyre full of holes! He probably flung them down the side of the mountain.'

They stood for a moment and Bob said quietly, 'You need help with this, Nick. Get on to the police.'

Nick nodded. 'I have, but I'm trying to keep Grace out of it.'

'That may not be possible,' Bob said.

Nick was quiet for a while. 'I couldn't live with myself if anything happened to Grace and the babies. The problem with this terrorist is that he's devious.'

Bob clapped him on the shoulder, bringing forth a yelp of pain. 'Sorry, mate. I was just going to suggest that you've been known to be devious yourself, so my money's on you to outsmart him.'

Nick grinned. 'I hope that you're right. Just at the moment, I think he's got the upper hand.'

Bob's eyes narrowed. 'We'll get him, Nick. That's a promise.'

As he left, Nick comforted himself that if anyone could track down his potential killer, it was Bob Fisher – ex-commando and boyhood friend.

The upheaval over the next few days prevented Grace from tackling Nick about the twins' parentage. He needed to have his car assessed and until he organised a hire car he borrowed her vehicle, using it to go to the factory in order to keep tabs on progress there. She was in no doubt that he had enough to cope with, and she also needed the time to let her emotions settle, enabling her to think clearly about the situation.

But even thinking about the future made her stomach lurch. For months she had seen Nick, the babies and herself as a compact little family. But now, because of a short conversation with Bob Fisher, that image had been shattered into a million fragments. She had trusted Karen implicitly, especially when she was so ill. And despite Karen's faults, it had never occurred to Grace that she would tell a lie about the father of her children. She shuddered as she thought about the number of times she had caught Karen out in a lie or a deception, realising just how foolish she had been to take her sister's word as the gospel truth.

She remembered how, when she had repeated Karen's claims, Nick had adamantly refused to accept that the babies were his – even declaring that he'd never had a relationship with Karen. She also recalled how she had brushed his protests aside, believing that he was merely reluctant to admit that the twins were his.

Nick certainly had his own problems. Despite his injuries, he was intending to overcome the obstacles to a future which he was now determined to spend with Grace and the babies. He thought of the phone call, preventing him from telling her that Sam was the twins' father, but the fall-out from his accident seemed to be taking up every minute of his time. He frowned as he realised that, despite her concern for his welfare, Grace never seemed to be readily available for a conversation – which clearly needed both time and discussion to have a positive outcome.

Strangely he didn't feel at risk driving to the factory, because on a weekday there was plenty of traffic. Besides, he knew that after a failed attempt, the man who appeared determined to put paid to his existence usually lay low.

He had alerted the police, who were hamstrung without any real proof, although a totally wrecked car and Nick's injuries went a long way towards convincing them. His first task was to question the man who'd rung him about the problem at the factory. The call had come from a reliable employee, and Nick couldn't believe that he was in cahoots with a criminal.

The machine he had rung about had indeed broken down, but on investigation they realised that it had been sabotaged. Which meant that the factory's security had been breached.

No doubt the man who wanted to see Nick dead, had

realised that a halt in production was guaranteed to bring Nick out on the road to the factory. And if Nick hadn't been lucky, the diabolical plan would have almost succeeded.

After a few days, Nick's injuries subsided and the backlash from the accident eased. Although he felt uneasy and desperately worried about Grace and the twins, he knew that he had done everything possible. Bob Fisher now had a couple of hefty workers, whose presence Nick explained away, by saying that he had some building projects to be done on the farm which involved heavy work.

However, once Nick had recovered and resumed his normal routine, Grace's thoughts centred on her own problems. The calm exterior which she presented to Nick when he came home each evening, hid a seething mass of emotions. She knew that they had to talk about the twins, but she couldn't find the courage to instigate the conversation. When Nick went straight to his office each evening after their meal, she found herself breathing a sigh of relief at the temporary reprieve.

At least her inability to sleep gave Grace time to plan her course of action. She had thought about her situation until her head ached, and one thing kept returning to torment her. She couldn't live on Nick's charity any longer. The fact that he had contributed so much to the twins' upbringing for the past few months left a legacy of guilt that would haunt her forever. Sure, the twins were his family – but, they were her family, too. And it seemed unfair that he should be providing all the financial support.

As she eased her exhausted body out of bed one morning, she realised that she had come full circle. She would have to go back to the sisters in Brisbane who had helped her, until she could find a teaching position and someone to care for the twins. At least if she did that, she could make some contribution to their welfare. Perhaps not an equal amount, of course, but at least a fair share of the money which would be required to bring them up. She felt sure that Nick would play his part as their uncle, but at least it would mean that he could get on with his life, without being totally tied to his brother's children.

Packing up and escaping had been impossible while Nick was injured. Nor had she been able to use her car. But now he had recovered his health, and had the use of a hired car until the new one he'd ordered was delivered. Even so, it was going to be no mean feat with a pair of watchdogs like Lucy and Bob. In two days, the twins were due for a check-up at the clinic and, although Lucy usually accompanied her, Grace asked her to stay behind and cook some meals for the twins.

'They go through solid food like a pair of baby vultures,' Grace said. 'I can't keep up the supply and you're such a good cook.'

Having been brought up to discourage waste, her conscience worried her – but it was the only excuse she could think of. Somehow, she couldn't see Nick eating pureed chicken and vegetables or caramel custard, but if he returned to his former eating patterns it wasn't an impossibility.

Packing the car was going to be another hurdle to overcome. However, problems at the factory kept Nick late the evening before she planned to leave, giving Grace an opportunity to pack the essentials for herself and the babies. Sometimes she thought all the cloak and dagger stuff was unnecessary, because there seemed no reason why Nick would want them to stay. He had accepted responsibility for Sam and Sally, but if she could provide practical care for them with his financial help, it was likely that he would be happy to get his life back on track once again.

All Grace could think of was quietly slipping out of his life and covering her tracks until she had a plan of action worked out, enabling her to show him that she was prepared to play the major role in the twins' upbringing.

'Good luck at the clinic.'

Lucy stood on the back steps waving as Grace drove away, with the twins safely buckled into their seats in the rear of the car. She didn't look back, but if she had, she would have been able to see nothing for the tears in her eyes. It was like leaving a piece of herself behind. She'd come to feel part of Nick's life. His home, Lucy, Bob and Dan had all enriched her life. Now she was going back to the beginning. To the stress and loneliness of being a single mother.

She was a little way along the road, when she caught a glimpse of Bob Fisher's vehicle in the rear view mirror. Damn! He was probably heading for the local township and if she turned off the road he would immediately become suspicious.

Forced by circumstances to do as she had claimed, Grace pulled into the car park belonging to the clinic, glad for once in her life that she didn't have a lot of possessions. At least the gear that she had packed for herself and the babies was mostly hidden in the boot and on the back seat. She'd had a few bad moments when Lucy had come to wave them off, but her position on the back steps had been too far away to see what was in the car.

The clinic sister made the usual fuss over Sam and Sally and reassured Grace that they were doing beautifully. As she changed their nappies, Grace felt the pangs of regret. Would they continue to thrive under changed circumstances and without the benefits which they had received since they'd been living with Nick?

She sighed. The benefits had been far more than financial. Whether he was their natural father or not, Nick had been a wonderful father figure for them. As she finished changing them she felt the first stirrings of doubt. Was she doing the right thing? The window in the clinic overlooked the main street and she could see Bob Fisher parked across the road, a short distance from the intersection.

She had the uneasy feeling that he was keeping tabs on her and she wondered if Nick had an inkling of what she had planned. Just as she was trying to work out an escape route, a car ran the red light and collided with another car at the intersection, pushing it into Bob Fisher's car.

He immediately jumped out of his car, becoming involved in a heated discussion with the driver of the offending vehicle. The owner of the car which had been pushed into Bob's, joined in the fray and it looked like becoming a real circus.

Grace didn't waste any more time pondering what she should do. She put the twins in the stroller and rushed out to the car park, leaving an astonished clinic sister in her wake. As she stowed the lightweight stroller and strapped the twins in, she thanked God for all the times she had performed the same ritual and the speed she had attained from practice.

Driving along the road, she kept an eye on both the rear view mirror and the speedometer. There was no sign of Bob when she turned off the road to Brisbane, and from what she'd seen of the damage to his car, it looked as though it would take him a while to get mobile again.

Nick glanced at his watch and picked up the phone. Grace was taking the children to the clinic today and she should be home by now. A grin hovered about his mouth. If someone had told him, only a few months ago, that he'd be anxious to know if two babies had gained weight and were thriving normally, he would have been ready to have them certified.

He could hear the phone ringing at the other end, and rapped his fingers on the shiny surface of his desk until Lucy answered it.

'Not back yet?' Nick glanced again at his watch. He would have expected Grace and the babies to have been home at least an hour earlier, but then he didn't know what plans Grace had for the rest of the day.

'Ask her to ring me when she comes in, Lucy, please.'

As he put the phone down, he felt a twinge of uneasiness, but quickly dismissed it as trivial. There had been no sign of the man who seemed hell bent on harming him, and Bob Fisher was keeping an eye on Grace and the twins. Becoming a family man took some getting used to and he was obviously just being over anxious. Images of Grace, and Sam and Sally danced through his mind. Suddenly, he realised that they meant everything to him.

He drew in a shocked breath as he gazed through the window to the busy throng on the factory floor. It was true! He'd thought that establishing his own business and at last having the freedom to do his own designing and manufacturing was his ultimate goal. But it all meant nothing in comparison to sharing his life with Grace and the twins.

He rocked back in his chair as his life slotted neatly into place, like the solving of a large and difficult puzzle. He felt a great surge of happiness as he realised that he now knew *exactly* what he wanted from life – and it all centred around a red-haired woman and two beautiful children. He closed his eyes for a moment. His brother's children, and he still hadn't said anything to Grace.

As far as he was concerned, they had become his own children weeks ago. The fact that they were Sam's babies made no difference to his feelings for them. Would that knowledge make a difference to Grace, and was that why he'd held off telling her? He had no idea, but he knew she could never bear to be parted from Sam and Sally – so that was something in his favour.

He opened his eyes, lowering his chair and rising to his feet, before putting on his jacket and grabbing up his brief-case. He could work at home. No! He wasn't going to do any more work that day. He needed to tell Grace how he felt about her and about Sam and Sally. He needed to be with her, and by the time he got home she should be there to greet him.

'Not here?' Nick threw a glance around the kitchen and settled a disgusted look on Lucy as if it was all her fault.

'No,' Lucy said, a worried frown creasing her brow. 'She would have left the clinic hours ago and she didn't say she was going shopping. Besides the twins will be hungry by now and she asked me to cook their meals for them.'

For a moment panic surged through Nick, but he battered it down. He knew that he was in an emotional state, with his feelings suddenly becoming clear and the discovery of the tremendous depth of his love for both Grace and the babies. A wave of nausea shot through him. What if he had found the loves of his life – only to lose them before he could tell them?

He leaned on the table, forcing himself to remain calm.
'They'll be home because... She was usually a tower of strength, but he could see she was ...came in from town and he says that he didn't leave the clinic, or any sign of her at the shop-

ping centre. His car was involved in an accident though, so I guess he was preoccupied with that.'

For a moment, feelings of panic surged through Nick, but he forced himself to be calm. 'What caused the accident to Bob's car?'

'I think a teenager ran a red light and hit a woman's car, which then clipped Bob's vehicle. It was just one of those annoying incidents.'

Nick frowned. It did sound like a run of the mill accident and Bob was trained to hone in on anything suspicious, but it still didn't explain Grace's absence. He knew he had to think positively.

'Lucy, stop worrying. As I said, I'm sure that they'll be home any time now.'

Slowly she shook her head. 'I'm not sure about that, Nick.'

Her worried look chilled his blood. 'What are you saying, Lucy?'

'Nick, just before you came in, I folded the washing and went to put it away. Grace's clothes are gone and so have most of the twins'. 'Their feeding bottles are also missing. She might have taken a couple with her, but she wouldn't have taken them all. I don't know why I didn't notice it earlier, but a lot of things are missing.'

Nick rushed through to the bedrooms, confirming what Lucy had told him. Obviously large items like the babies' cots provided still there. In fact, most of the stuff he had chord. He lowered his head in his hands and that immediately struck a and dreams. Shattered down on to her bed and dropped gone. All his hopes

chapter fifteen

As the days went by with no news and no contact from Grace, Nick felt as if he'd go mad. To find the love of his life, his reason for being – and then to have the whole thing snatched away – left a great empty void. His way of coping was to subject any individual who'd had the slightest contact with Grace to a third degree, which would have done the Spanish Inquisition proud – and then to totally lose patience with them when they couldn't help.

Never one to pussy-foot around, Bob Fisher cornered him one morning. 'You need to back off,' he said. 'You'll never find Grace this way. In fact you'll drive her further underground.'

'What the hell do you mean, "underground"? If you knew Grace as well as I do, you'd know that no one, least of all me, can drive her to do anything she doesn't want to.'

'She obviously wanted to leave,' Bob said. 'I told you, not telling her about Sam being their father was a mistake.'

Nick eyeballed Bob belligerently. 'I suppose you think that your little effort in spilling the beans was a good idea?'

Bob looked uncomfortable. 'I've apologised for that. It was just a slip in a moment of tension. Life hasn't been exactly stable around here, with someone taking pot shots at you and the police and private detectives stirring up the dust.'

Nick let out a heartfelt sigh. 'I know. I worry that something has happened to them. I've lost them, Bob.'

Bob put a large hand on his shoulder. 'Let me find them, Nick. Now that you've told me about Grace's background, I'm sure that she will have turned to the church for help.'

Nick nodded. As Bob left he felt an easing of the terrible stress under which he'd been labouring. Bob was right. He couldn't think or act rationally when he was so emotionally involved, and life had to go on. The factory was still his responsibility and the people he employed relied on him to keep it viable.

The nights were the worst and when he did eat, he reverted to his terrible eating habits. Mostly he looked at the food and then threw it out in disgust. Wandering around the house only underlined his depression, and he inevitably ended up working in his office to keep his thoughts from going around in circles.

Even so, he had analysed every aspect of the events which had occurred before Grace did a runner. Could she have sensed that she and the twins were in danger? Even if she had, he didn't think that she'd react the way she had. Surely she would have said something?

His gut feeling was that it was probably the discovery about Sam being the father of the twins, plus the fact that he hadn't told her. He drew in a deep breath. That would have been a shattering discovery, throwing a whole new light on the situation. She had said once that she didn't trust him – and the fact that he had withheld the truth would only have reinforced that distrust. He had no choice but to hope and pray that she would contact him when she got herself together again.

As he climbed into bed after filling in another interminable day, Nick gave up trying to contain his thoughts and let them wander at will. There was so much he needed to explain to Grace – and much that he didn't have a clear picture of himself. He was still seeing the counsellor, who was helping him put his life together again after the emotional setbacks which he'd sustained over the years. She was the only one who could help him sort out his problems. Or was she?

No! She damn well wasn't! There was one other person who could help him get his life back on track. And although that person was just about the last person he could reach out to, he was going to do it anyway. He sat up on the side of the bed, reached out for the phone and rang his father.

Nick guided the big vehicle along the highway towards Brisbane, his thoughts ranging back over the events of the past few days. Ringing his father had indeed been like reaching for a lifeline and, to his astonishment, he'd discovered that his father also needed that lifeline. So intense was their need to communicate, that he'd dressed and set off to see his father straight away; driving through the night, sleep forgotten.

When he'd arrived at the farm, his father had made coffee and toast and they'd sat and talked. Thinking back over that amazing conversation, Nick realised that so much suffering could have been avoided if they'd both reached out years before. But Sam had been alive then and, paradoxically, it was his brother's death which had helped to bridge the gulf which lay between his father and himself. Now they could both see things from each other's perspective. They both realised that although the past couldn't be undone, it was now time to think about the future.

The future. Those words reverberated through Nick's mind. That's where he was headed. To see Grace. To cement his future. While there were no guarantees that he would succeed, he refused to think in terms of failure. He'd suffered much rejection in his life, but if Grace rejected him he didn't know how he would cope.

His hands tightened on the steering wheel, a wry grin twisting his mouth. She'd wormed her way right into the inner core of him and now he would be begging her to return to him. Well if that's what it took – that's what he would do! He reached the turn off and he took a deep breath before entering the gates of the retreat.

Two weeks had seemed like a lifetime. Grace, sitting beneath a shady tree with the twins besides her, tried unsuccessfully to quell the depression which had recently become so much a part of her existence.

The sisters had welcomed her back, establishing her at one of their retreats in a Brisbane suburb with the quiet acceptance which stemmed from their lifestyle and their faith. She realised that she was only marking time. It was imperative that she started earning a living. In order to do that, she knew that she would have to find a reliable person to mind the twins while she returned to teaching. At least they were older now, and over a few of the hurdles which she had faced when they were tiny babies.

Sally and Sam had fallen asleep on their blanket and Grace stood up to stretch her legs. The old house, now used as the retreat, was situated up on a hill. As she looked out over the spectacular scenery below, Grace felt the calm beauty of the lush green bush-land and the sounds of birds and insects seeping into her troubled mind and helping to lift her depression.

She stood for several minutes, eventually turning her gaze towards the long drive that wound up from the road. It was mostly a rough track and the car that made its way towards the house was almost obscured in a cloud of dust. Although she didn't recognise the car, the fact that it was a big four-wheel drive vehicle triggered memories which she had tried so hard to eradicate. It couldn't be Nick.

Tracing her would have been extremely difficult, if not impossible.

For a moment, she felt a surge of guilt. There was no question in her mind that he was fond of Sam and Sally, and she should at least have let him know that they were safe.

The car stopped a short distance away – and then her hand was flying to her mouth in shock as she saw Nick striding towards her. For a moment, she thought that he was going to pull her into his arms, but he stopped short his hands extended towards her.

'Why?' He drew in an agonised breath. '*Why* did you run away, Gracie? You must know I would never have done anything to hurt you or the twins!'

'Hurt us?' She felt as if they were communicating from two different planets. 'Of course, I know that. But…but, there are degrees of hurting, Nick, and once I knew for sure that Sally and Sam weren't yours, I knew that any hope of our future together was shattered.'

'*Not mine…*?' he roared. 'What are you talking about? *Of course, they're mine!*'

She shook her head. Dear God – he was still refusing to tell her the truth.

'I know that they belong to your brother Sam. Bob Fisher told me.'

The scene which he'd had with Bob, when the other man had confessed to committing the indiscretion of alerting Grace to the twins' true parentage, flashed into his mind. Nick's colourful description of what he intended to do to that individual, had made even the stoical ex-commando wince. But, in the end, friendship had won out and Bob had proved to be a valuable asset in tracing Grace.

'Yes, they are Sam's children. But Sam is dead and, as far as I'm concerned, that makes them mine. How could you take them away from me, Grace? Why did you do it?'

Grace twisted her hands together to stop them from trembling. In her stressed state of mind, it seemed that she'd got everything wrong. He looked haggard and tired. Giving him back his life or his freedom, as she'd been so intent on doing, hadn't done a thing for his well-being. He looked like a man who'd been to hell and back.

She raised her eyes to Nick as he took her hands in his. His strength seemed to flow through her, calming her fluttering heart and giving her courage.

'Then you accept Sally and Sam as your children?' She held her breath. 'You want to play a part in their upbringing? More than financial support.'

'Grace, from the moment I knew that they were Sam's children, I've regarded them as my own.' He hesitated. 'I admit it took some coming to terms with. But, as for loving them, I think that happened the minute I laid eyes on them. I'd never thought of myself as a father and, quite frankly Gracie, I was running scared. That's why I didn't tell you as soon as I knew the truth. I needed time to adjust, and then…then it seems that I left it all too late.' He explained why Bob had thought that she must have known that Sam was the twins' father, when he'd made the comment he did.

'But, how did you know? The detective…? You were having their background investigated?'

'Wrong – Miss Sticky Beak! The detective had nothing to do with the twins.'

She *was* living on another planet. Surely it was the only explanation?

Nick sat down on the edge of the blanket, pulling her down beside him. He left a little distance between them, but kept her hand in his.

'I think we need to sort out a few things,' he told her

firmly. 'I won't deny that I've kept certain things from you, but I honestly felt that it was the right thing to do at the time.'

Grace tried to marshal her rampaging thoughts. 'Then, if you weren't investigating the twins' background, I don't understand why you needed to hire a private detective.' She drew in a sharp breath. 'Was it me you were having investigated?'

'No, Gracie, it was not you. I've suspected for a long time that the person who threw that rock at us, and who started the fire on the property – and who, incidentally, also caused the accident which wrote off my car – was someone with a personal vendetta against me. I couldn't trace the person I suspected, so I got a detective to do it for me.'

'But, who would try to kill you?'

Unconsciously, Nick rubbed a hand over the scar on his neck. 'The same man who took a shot at me in Saudi Arabia.'

Grace bit back a scream. He wasn't joking. Someone really *had* tried to kill him! And to kill her and the babies. It was almost beyond her conception that such people really existed.

Nick hastened to reassure her. 'It's OK, Grace. Thanks to the diligence of the police and Bob Fisher, he's now behind bars and about to be deported.'

'But, why would he come to Australia to carry on a personal feud?'

'I was in charge of a communications project in Saudi Arabia, that effectively destroyed the plans which he and his terrorist mates were hell bent on carrying out. He tried to dissuade me, and also tried to sabotage the project – even to the extent of involving Sam and ultimately causing Sam's accident. But we still managed to outsmart him and bring the project to completion. Which is why he apparently decided to come out here and try to finish me off.'

He took a deep steadying breath. 'I could never find the words to tell you, Grace, about the hell I went through with that project. I had to finish it, even though I had lost my brother, and then I almost lost my own life in an assassination attempt. It will always feature as just about the worst year of my life.'

Grace shuddered. 'Don't!' She took a deep breath as she tried to come to terms with what might have happened. Suddenly the pieces seemed to slot into place, giving her a clear picture of the past events.

'Bob Fisher,' she said. 'He wasn't just a landscape gardener, was he?'

Nick smiled as he shook his head. 'Ex-member of a Commando Unit of the Australian Army and long time friend. We were at boarding school together. He's retired from the army after a pretty impressive career.'

'Isn't he rather young to have retired?'

'He was injured in a parachute accident, and is now unfit for the unit which he belonged to. He preferred to retire, rather than take on a more mundane role.'

Grace smiled. 'I wonder how he'd feel about the role of Lucy's boyfriend?'

Nick put his arm around her shoulders. 'I think he's already auditioned for that role and been accepted. However, now that we've got Bob sorted out, I think we have a few things to sort out ourselves.'

He looked nervously around him. 'This is a convent isn't it?'

Grace smiled. 'It's a retreat.' She put her hand up and touched his arm where it rested on her shoulder. 'A display of affection is not forbidden.'

He turned her face towards him. 'I want you to come

home, Gracie.'

She looked into his face, trying to assess his reasons for wanting her to return. There were the babies, of course. He'd said that he accepted them as his own. And then she remembered seeing him at the medical centre.

'How did you find out that Sam was the twins' father? Did the DNA test you had throw any light on their parentage?'

His mouth dropped open and he tried to speak, but the words seemed lodged in his throat. 'DNA?' he croaked. 'What DNA test?'

She shrugged. 'I saw you going into the medical centre. I'd wondered why you didn't take the test and then I presumed that you'd decided to have it done.'

He shook his head. 'Gracie, you should try your hand at writing a novel. Your imagination is incredible. The fact is that I was going to see a counsellor about my past, and the effect it was having on my future, and she just happens to hang out in the medical centre with the other health professionals. I've had several sessions, which have all been very rewarding.'

She put her hands on his shoulders, gazing up into his eyes. 'Oh, Nick, I'm *so* glad you took that step. I know it couldn't have been easy for you.'

'Easier than the thought of losing you.' He hesitated for a moment. 'And I thought that I had.'

Grace held her breath. Did he mean…?

He looked into her eyes, his own mirroring the love that shone from hers. 'I love you Gracie. I'd give my life for you and the twins – but, I'd rather share it with you, Sally and Sam for the next fifty years or so.'

Her arms slid from his shoulders and tightened around his neck as her lips sought his.

All the love she felt for him flowed through that kiss,

and as his lips melded with hers she felt his love for her flowing back. It was as if they were one person, and it was the most wonderful feeling she had ever experienced. He turned her slightly, lifting her on to his lap, cradling her and holding her closely to him, as if he was afraid that she would disappear from his life, once again.

'Marry me, Gracie. I need you with me…beside me. Without you, my life has no meaning.'

'Yes,' she whispered. 'Yes! Yes! *Yes!*'

She felt the breath which he'd been holding, ease out of his lungs and his arms tightened. He looked over at the sleeping babies.

'You're getting a package deal.' He looked into her eyes. 'Sure you can cope?'

'With one hand tied behind my back,' she said. She glanced at the twins and a question still teased at the back of her mind.

'So, what *did* convince you that Sam was their father? Karen didn't mention Sam – which seems odd when they obviously had a relationship.'

He shook his head. 'I knew nothing about their relationship either, but because I had never at any stage had any kind of relationship with Karen – sexual or otherwise – I knew that the twins couldn't be mine. The only interaction I had with Karen was in the work sense. But I now realise that she and Sam must have met socially, because by then Sam was working with my company.'

He hesitated. 'I have since managed to confirm their relationship, because Sam took Karen to meet my father. He told me about it, when we spoke recently.'

Grace looked up at him quickly. 'You've spoken with your father? Recently?'

He gave her a crooked smile. 'Yes, a few days ago. I was beside myself with worry. I was trying to find you, but I had promised the counsellor that I would try to sort a few things out within my own family. She felt that until I did so, I wasn't going to completely resolve my problems. She also helped me cope with the fact that I had discovered how much I loved you – and just how shattered I was at losing you. She seemed confident that everything would come right – and it has!'

'With your father?' Grace spoke the words tentatively, hoping she wasn't opening any wounds.

'Oh yes. We laid everything out on the table, Grace. It was unbelievably difficult for both of us, but now we are beginning again. There is a lot of baggage from the past, of course, however we're both doing our best to discard it.'

'What kind of baggage? Emotional?'

'Very. I will always feel that I made a very bad decision in taking Sam to the Middle East. But I did it with the best of intentions, and both my father and I have to accept that.

'There is so much more between us, Grace. My father adored Sam, but he barely tolerated me and it hurt. Uncle Will, my father's older brother, was more of a father figure to me and it was only in recent years that I began to suspect why.'

Grace held her breath, her thoughts way ahead of him. 'He was your…'

Nick nodded. 'Yes, it turns out that he was my real father. Apparently he and my mother met and fell in love, before Will went off to the Antarctic for eighteen months. He was out of communication – and even if he could have been contacted, he couldn't return. In those days, they went in by icebreaker and came out the same way. There were no short cuts. Just after he left, my mother discovered that she was pregnant with Will's child. My father had always been in love with her and so he married her, but he could never extend that love to the child which had been conceived by another man.'

'Oh Nick!' She threw her arms around him and held him tightly to her. He was such a wonderful man, and he'd been given so little love in his life. And they had so much in common. She'd had a sister who had used her shamelessly, and yet she had loved Karen. Just as Nick had shown Sam equal love, even though Sam had displaced him in his family's affections.

Nick eased back slightly and she sensed that he needed to continue to explain; to purge all the secrets of his past. Talking it through would help him get things into perspective, and she hoped it would help to heal the deep wounds which he'd suffered through no fault of his own. However, she was surprised when he began speaking about his mother and empathising with her situation. How could he excuse her behaviour and the effect it had on his life?

'She was in a no-win situation, Grace. With hindsight, I now believe that she was afraid to love me for fear of upsetting my father, but there were times when she looked at me with tears in her eyes and I'm sure that she wanted to show me her true feelings. I think that by letting Will spend so much time with me, she felt that she was compensating for the love which I missed out on in our family situation.'

'Do you think Will knew that you were his son?'

Nick nodded. 'I believe so, but he'd obviously agreed to keep that knowledge to himself. My father married my mother to save her from becoming a single mother, at a time when that sort of situation was still frowned upon. And also because he loved her. When Will came back from the Antarctic, I think he had no choice but to go along with the whole arrangement. It was too late to change anything, and if he had recognised me as his son the situation for my mother would still have caused her severe distress.'

Nick shook his head as if to clear his thoughts. He smiled. 'About Sam. I know I said I don't have photos of myself from my childhood, but I do have some of Sam and his little twin is his spitting image.'

She hugged him tightly. 'That must have been difficult for you.'

'It caused a whole cauldron of emotion and at first I fought it until…'

'Until…?' she prompted.

'Until one day, when I picked up his little hand and I knew for certain. It was a shock.'

Grace frowned. She had no idea what he was talking about.

He eased her from his lap and sat beside Sam's sleeping form. Gently he picked up the little boy's hand and teased his fingers open.

'Look at his little finger,' he said. 'The other hand is the same.'

Sam's little fingers were slightly bent. Instead of standing straight up they curved towards the adjoining finger.

'I know,' Grace said. 'When he was born the paediatrician pointed it out, but he said it was genetic and wasn't a problem. He said there was probably someone in the family with bent little fingers.'

'There is,' Nick said. 'My father had them and so did Sam.' With a rueful smile he held his own straight fingered hands out. 'I haven't got them – but then, Will didn't have them either.'

'I remember,' Grace said. 'I remember one day, when you stood by the cot looking at Sam for ages. I wondered what you were thinking.'

He nodded. 'I was thinking how wonderful it was to

have a son and a daughter, even if they are really my niece and nephew. But what is far more important, Grace, is how wonderful it is to have *you* to love and cherish. If the twins hadn't been Sam's, I'd still have wanted them because they belong with you – and you, my darling, belong with me.'

chapter sixteen

Nick in organising mode was quite formidable. After meeting the sisters who had been so supportive to Grace, and the priest – the 'father who enjoyed a beer' – he arranged to return in a few weeks to marry Grace.

'You and the babies will come home with me, Gracie,' he said. 'We can come back when the required time to wait for a licence is up.' Correctly interpreting the priest's challenging look he hastened to reassure him. 'I have to make a trip overseas in the meantime and I promise you that separate bedrooms will be the order of the day.' He grinned. 'No sleepwalking either.'

Satisfied, the priest shook his hand and they set off for the Sunshine Coast.

'Overseas?' Grace felt a sense of disappointment. She didn't want to spend a minute apart from him, but she knew he wouldn't go unless it was necessary. A thought flitted into her mind and terrified her.

'Nick, you're not going to Saudi Arabia are you? To give evidence against that man.'

He laughed. 'No, darling. I'm going to Germany to ensure that I keep my hands off you until our wedding.'

'Oh!' She joined in the laughter. 'I guess Father Joe is a bit intimidating.'

He shook his head. 'No. Your feelings and ideals are important to me.' He gave her a rueful smile. 'I've got a lot to learn about putting other people first, but I've never been a slow learner.'

'You've never been as selfish as you make out either,

Nick. I think your biggest enemy has been fear.'

He nodded. 'Crazy isn't it? A great lump like me afraid of my own feelings. Not any more, Gracie. Not any more.' He took a hand off the steering wheel and picked up her hand placing a kiss in the palm. 'I adore you.' Gently he put her hand back on her lap as he used both hands to guide the big vehicle along the busy highway.

'Nick, how did you find me? The retreat isn't well known, and I didn't ever mention the area I lived in before.'

'Bob Fisher.' Nick smiled. 'He's a man of many parts. Tough soldier, loves speed and adventure and believes deeply in his religion.'

Grace looked at him in surprise. 'Really?'

'He knows many of the priests in Brisbane. It took him a little while, but he eventually tracked down the retreat where he felt you might have taken refuge.' He turned towards her smiling. 'When you left, we talked and he realised he had let slip about the babies being Sam's. He was devastated and wouldn't rest until he found you.'

He glanced quickly at her smiling, before he returned his attention to the road. 'Bob and I go way back.' He hesitated for a moment. 'He's more than just a school friend. He's been one of the mainstays in my life. When everything else seemed to lack substance, security, I knew that his friendship was rock solid and that he'd never let me down.

'Although I had Will in the background, there were long periods of time when he was working away from Australia. In those times Bob was there to listen, to advise and to be my backstop.'

She thought about what he told her, realising more than he knew about what it took to reveal the insecurities of his childhood, and how he had managed to cope with them. He was a strong man, but even strong men can need help and she was glad that Bob had always been there for him. A mental picture of Bob flashed into her mind. Big, gruff and apparently a man of enormously strong convictions and character.

She turned towards him. 'I hope Lucy can cope with all that.'

Nick smiled. 'Lucy can cope with anything. Bob's just the man for her. A bit older, but I don't think that matters. Do you?'

She detected the thread of anxiety. 'No. Age doesn't matter when you love someone.'

'There's more than ten years between us, love.'

'And of course there's that silver streak in your hair,' she joked.

'Never mind that,' he said. 'All the important bits are in fine fettle!'

'Nick,' she said, shocked. 'How do you know?'

'Because they've been giving me problems – ever since you turned up on my doorstep. So, if you don't stop teasing, I'll be tempted to give you a demonstration.'

'Remember Father Joe,' she said.

'How could I forget!'

Deep down, Grace knew that Nick's absence had nothing to do with Father Joe – and everything to do with his love for her. Although she missed him, there was so much to do that the weeks flew by. In fact, it seemed that in no time at all, she was standing in front of the mirror in her wedding gown.

Lucy, her bridesmaid, had insisted that she dress for the wedding at her parents' home. Lucy's mother had offered to look after Sam and Sally, taking them home after the ceremony was over.

'I don't know how we would have managed to get

married at all without you and your family,' Grace said. 'Are you sure you don't mind having the twins here for the whole weekend?'

'Grace, Dan and Bob are both going to help. You and Nick should be having a real honeymoon. You know, a couple of weeks at least.'

'We can do that later on. Now we just want to be together as husband and wife, and parents of course.'

'You've always been a family,' Lucy said. 'It just took Nick a while to get his act together. He'll make a wonderful husband and father.'

As they took their vows in the church in Brisbane, Grace thought about Lucy's words. Both she and Nick had done a lot of soul searching over the last few months, realising that they'd found their role in life and, more importantly, that they'd found each other.

As they turned to walk back down the aisle after becoming man and wife, Grace gazed around at the people who had come to see them married. New friends, wonderful friends. She bit back a smile as Dan sat in the front row, Sam on his lap, chatting to Lucy's mother who held Sally.

While she watched, a man with dark hair liberally sprinkled with grey, put out his arms and took Sam. Nick's father. Not his biological father, of course, but she knew deep in her heart that he would now regard Nick as his son and the father of his grandchildren. They were bound together by tragedy and the regret that it took that tragedy to forge a true bond between them. But they were willing to work at their relationship, both for their own sakes and that of the two little children.

Whatever enmity had been between Nick and Dan seemed to be resolved. Lucy had told her that Dan had played his part in keeping an eye out for the terrorist, and any devious plans he might try to put into practice.

Their reception was held in the church hall, Nick realising that much love and caring for Grace had gone into the preparations. The wedding dress she wore was stunning in its simplicity – enhancing the soft curves which happiness and contentment had added to her slender beauty during the weeks leading up to their wedding. The picture of joy and goodness which she presented made his heart ache with love for her.

'I need to change into street clothes,' she whispered as the last of their well-wishers disappeared.

'Me too,' he said running a finger around the tight collar of his formal shirt.

Fifteen minutes later they took their leave. Dressed in comfortable slacks and shirts, they climbed into Nick's new vehicle to make the trip to Sanctuary Cove near the Queensland Gold Coast.

Nick glanced across at Grace. She turned towards him with a serene smile. He felt his heart turn over with the love he felt for her. She was his life and he would love and care for her until the day he died.

A small frown puckered his brow. He hadn't lied when he'd said that his body had responded to her from the moment of laying eyes on her. Now that physical need was overlaid with the love he felt, he wanted everything to be perfect for her. He let out a deep sigh. He'd never lacked confidence in the bedroom before, but then he hadn't bedded innocent virgins who looked like a puff of air could blow them away.

'That's a fearsome frown, Mr Best.'

'Concentrating on the road, Mrs Best.'

'You're lying, Nick.'

He gasped at her perception.

She put her hand on his knee and squeezed. 'Whatever it is, it's going to be all right.'

He almost laughed aloud. His body's immediate and volatile reaction to her touch definitely didn't bode for an 'all right' situation. He had to get himself under control and quickly. He turned the conversation back to their reception and managed to beat his rampant hormones into some kind of submission.

By the time they reached their destination and were established in their luxury suite, he'd managed to calm his shattered nervous system.

A lengthy spell under the shower gave him some breathing space, and when he emerged Grace was standing in front of the huge window looking at the night sky.

She turned towards him and he caught his breath. Bright red curls, grown much longer now, framed her lovely face and contrasted with the cream, silky night-dress she wore. It clung to the soft curves of her body, and he said a prayer of thanks for her new contentment and increased appetite. Secure in his love for her and the twins, she radiated a happiness which he never wanted to see diminished. He drew in a deep breath. She meant everything to him. She was his life!

All the benefits gained from the shower disappeared in seconds.

'I was star gazing,' she said.

'Making a wish,' he guessed, surprised when she shook her head.

'Why should I? All my wishes have come true.'

'All of them, Gracie?'

'One to go,' she whispered throwing her arms around his neck.

He swung her up into his arms. He felt ten feet tall. The worries that had plagued him melted away in the knowledge that his love for Grace would guide him. It might be the first time for Grace, but it was a new experience for him – because he had never before experienced the depth of love and devotion which he felt for Grace.

She felt like thistledown in his arms and her kisses tasted like honey. There wasn't a hint of nervousness about her reactions to his gentle explorations, and even when he removed both her clothes and his, she smiled at him making little noises of pleasure as they finally touched skin to skin. The ironclad control which he'd imposed on himself took a beating, as she surprised him with a passion he wouldn't have dreamed was lurking beneath her quiet exterior. He felt as if he was drowning in ecstasy, but he forced himself to hold on.

For a man who had shunned love, he was now overwhelmed with it. The unison it brought between him and Grace, both in body and soul almost robbed him of breath. It was in total harmony that they joined their bodies and together made the journey to the joyous climax of their love.

For Nick it had been everything – and far more than he had ever dreamed of. He drew Grace into the shelter of his arms, gently kissing her forehead. There were no words to express how he felt. He hoped that she knew.

Grace wondered if the thunderous beat of her heart would ever settle. Nothing in her life had ever touched her so deeply. She and Nick were truly one and always would be. How could she have ever compared him to his namesake? Under the harsh exterior that he presented to the world, was a man who really cared. And, having learned how to love, he would do it the way he did everything – with all his heart and soul.

Her body sang from his tender touches and she felt complete as she had never felt before. If there had been any discomfort, it had been lost in the pleasure of sharing her body with Nick. She turned her head and kissed the side of his neck, her lips stretching in a smile.

'I know you're smiling,' Nick said. 'Now I wonder just what that means.'

'It means I love you,' Grace whispered. 'I think I always have – right from the first moment I saw you.'

Nick chuckled. 'It's the same with me. But I never expected to be introduced to love on my own doorstep.'

Grace laughed, thinking of the twins. He'd got a triple dose of love.

Nick turned her face up to his kissing her on the lips. 'What's so funny?'

'It wasn't just love on a doorstep,' Grace said. 'It was love by Special Delivery!'

Heartline Books
Romance at its best

Why not discover more exciting romances from Heartline? If you have missed any books so far from Heartline, it's so easy to order them directly, either by calling
the Heartline Hotline on 0845 6000504 or by visiting our
website at www.heartlinebooks.com. There you will also
find competitions, special free book offer, and your very
own reader's page. All of the following titles published
to date by Heartline are still currently available:

The Windrush Affairs *by Maxine Barry*	£3.99
Soul Whispers *by Julia Wild*	£3.99
Beguiled *by Kay Gregory*	£3.99
Red Hot Lover *by Lucy Merritt*	£3.99
Stay Very Close *by Angela Drake*	£3.99
Jack of Hearts *by Emma Carter*	£3.99
Destiny's Echo *by Julie Garrett*	£3.99
The Truth Game *by Margaret Callaghan*	£3.99
His Brother's Keeper *by Kathryn Bellamy*	£3.99
Never Say Goodbye *by Clare Tyler*	£3.99
Fire Storm *by Patricia Wilson*	£3.99
Altered Images *by Maxine Barry*	£3.99
Yesterday's Man *by Natalie Fox*	£3.99
Running for Cover *by Harriet Wilson*	£3.99
Moth to the Flame *by Maxine Barry*	£3.99
Second Time Around *by June Ann Monks*	£3.99
Melting the Iceman *by Maxine Barry*	£3.99
Marrying a Stranger *by Sophie Jaye*	£3.99
Secrets *by Julia Wild*	£3.99

Tell us what you think!

Because we want to make sure that we continue to offer you books which are up to the high standard you expect, we need to know a little more about *you* and your reading likes and dislikes. So please spare a few moments to fill in the questionnaire on the following pages and send it back to us.

Questionnaire

Please tick the boxes to indicate your answers:

1 Did you enjoy reading this Heartline book?

Title of book: _____

A lot ☐
A little ☐
Not at all ☐

2 What did you particularly like about this book?

Title of book: _____

Believable characters ☐
Easy to read ☐
Good value for money ☐
Enjoyable locations ☐
Interesting story ☐
Favourite author ☐
Modern setting ☐

3 If you didn't like this book, can you please tell us why?

_____

_____

4 What other kinds of books do you enjoy reading?

Puzzle books ☐
Crime/Detective fiction ☐
Non-fiction ☐

Other _____

5 Which magazines and/or newspapers do you read regularly?

a) _____

b) _____

c) _____

d) _____

6 Our books can be ordered directly from us at www.heartlinebooks.com and we are always interested to know what you would like to see on our website:

a) Exclusive celebrity/author interviews?

   Interested ☐   Not Interested ☐

b) Competitions, puzzles etc?

   Interested ☐   Not Interested ☐

c) Special offers?

   Interested ☐   Not Interested ☐

d) Readers' letters?

   Interested ☐   Not Interested ☐

What else would you like to see on our website?

_____

_____

_____

And now a bit about you:

Name _____

Address _____

_____

_____ Postcode _____

We may use this information to send you offers from
ourselves or selected companies, which may be of
interest to you. If you prefer not to receive such offers,
please tick this box ☐

Thank you so much for completing this questionnaire.
Now just tear it out and send it in an envelope to:

HEARTLINE BOOKS
FREEPOST LON 16243
Swindon SN2 8LA

(If you don't want to spoil this book, please feel free to
write to us at the above address with your comments
and opinions.)

Heartline Books...

Romance at its best™